John Jeremiah

An Aid to Shakespearean Study

.

John Jeremiah

An Aid to Shakespearean Study

ISBN/EAN: 9783337403348

Printed in Europe, USA, Canada, Australia, Japan

Cover: Foto ©Andreas Hilbeck / pixelio.de

More available books at **www.hansebooks.com**

AN

Aid to Shakespearean Study.

BY

JOHN JEREMIAH,

(MEMBER OF THE ANTHROPOLOGICAL INSTITUTE OF GREAT BRITAIN
AND IRELAND),

(Author of NOTES ON SHAKESPEARE, *and* MEMORIALS OF THE URBAN
CLUB, *&c.)*

LONDON:

H. SOTHERAN & Co., 77 and 78, Queen Street, E.C.; Eastcheap, E.C.;
146, Strand, W.C.; and 36, Piccadilly, S.W.
—
1880.

TO

Jonas Levy, Esq.,

WHOSE MANY ACTS OF KINDNESS AND ENCOURAGEMENT

HAVE LAID ME UNDER A DEEP SENSE OF

INDEBTEDNESS,

I DEDICATE

This Book,

WITH HEARTFELT

GRATITUDE.

JOHN JEREMIAH.

FOREWORDS.

HE spread of Shakespearean Literature, especially of recent years, and the consequent growth of controversy regarding the views of every new exponent of the works and text of the great dramatist, have become matters of such magnitude, that the student, and indeed the casual reader, may stand aghast, or fly the arena of Shakespearean criticism, and seek sweet solace in the simple, but perhaps archaic, text of the FIRST FOLIO, with a resolution to pass over the words now obsolete or misprinted, and rely upon one's own interpretation of the poet's meaning of passages that may appear obscure or involuted; such a spirit of resignation is highly commendable, but there is something to be said on the side of the commentators and elucidators. The Text of the quarto and folio editions of the separate and collected plays, fairly admits of critical examination. Words are used that have no apparent meaning in the form therein printed; and the quarto and folio versions do not always agree. Excisions and additions have been made, that tend to further beautify the mode or form of expression; passages from previous writers, occur in the plays, that manifestly show that Shakespeare adapted, assimilated, and endowed with a life and grace unknown before his time; the rough and faded sketch was touched, and form and beauty stepped from the canvas to captivate the mind of man for all time. The Sources of the plays form a separate branch of enquiry, and can hardly be ignored, even by the most irascible opponent of Shakespearean criticism. To know from whence Shakespeare gleaned the outlines of many of his plots, enlarges one's knowledge of literary and general history, and brings one into closer communion with the traditions, mythical or real, that were current in, and before, his day. Novels and popular historical tales were alike made to supply materials for the glorious edifice he was building up, and critical as we may be, and chary of

assenting to a belief in the solidity of the mere gossamer of mediæval fiction and superstition, yet, when looked at through the medium of Shakespeare, we feel a new interest in the fables of the early chroniclers and story-tellers, and would fain accept that which, handled by another hand, would be rejected as mere figments and waifs of a dark and ignorant age.

It is hoped then that sufficient reasons have been adduced, for kindly tolerating the existence of the immense company of commentators and elucidators, and the beginner in, if not the pronounced student of, Shakespearean Study may do well to look into the books of such writers, and sift, where possible, the corn from the chaff; to aid such, the following HAND LIST has been drawn up. with such remarks upon the books and articles relating more or less to the life and works of the dramatist, that may serve as a guide. Obviously, the scope being extensive, many items of importance have to be looked for, in books especially, that do not indicate by their titles the contents, so far as the object here treated of is concerned; these are included in their place, according to date. As regards miscellaneous (periodical) literature, hundreds of magazines and weekly journals have been ransacked, and those of any transient or permanent importance are herein given, with reference to year and day, and in many cases the gist of an article or communication is given in *epitome*, and commented upon, with as little bias as possible. [1]

In an object of this character, it is not made of first importance to give a bibliography of Shakespeare; many works are necessarily omitted, and many others will occur to the reader; for instance—Mrs. Cowden Clarke's *Concordance to the Plays of Shakespeare* is not given, but every student should possess it; the *Cambridge Shakespeare*, which is valuable for its readings of quartos, folios, and subsequent editions, should be consulted in conjunction with Mr. H. H. Furness's *Variorum Shakespeare*; so far as the latter has proceeded, reference to which will be found under 1873 in the LIST OF WORKS. For the meanings of words, etc., Schmidt's *Shakespeare Lexicon* is indispensable; and to obtain an idea of England in the Elizabethan era, the valuable edition of William Harrison's *Description of England* (*New Shakspere Society Publication*, 1877) should be consulted.

---

[1] The Magazines and Weekly Journals examined, are those issued within the past *sixteen* years.

The scope of this little book does not strictly comprehend the study of the Pre-Shakespearean Drama, but for those desirous of working in this field the following works are recommended :—

A Dissertation on the Pageants or Dramatic Mysteries Anciently performed at Coventry, &c., by T. Sharp. 1825.

The Towneley Mysteries. Being Vol. 1 of *The Surtees Society's Publications.* 1836.

A Collection of English Miracle-Plays or Mysteries, &c., by by William Marriott, Ph. D. 1838.

The Skryvener's Play, The Incredulity of St. Thomas. Edited by J. Payne Collier, Esq., F.S.A. 1859. Being Vol. IV. of *The Camden Miscellany.* *Camden Society's Publication.*

Interesting accounts of the Miracle-Plays will also be found in Ulrici's *Shakspeare's Art,* given in the LIST OF WORKS under 1876; The *Ober-Ammergau Passion Play,* by the Rev. Malcolm Mac Coll, M.A., 1880, (*vide, Introduction*), *Miracle Plays and Sacred Dramas: An Historical Survey,* by Dr. Karl Hase, Trans. by A. W. Jackson, and edited by the Rev. W. W. Jackson, 1880. Hone's *Ancient Mysteries* (sub. 1823), and Halliwell's, *Ludus Coventriæ,* (1841 *vide,* Note to *Kemp,* 1840 in LIST OF WORKS,) may also be added to this list. These works will be found invaluable, as they really contain, with the volume of the *Chester Plays,* Edited by T. Wright, (*Old Shakespeare Society's Publication* 1843), all that is to be said on this branch of study. [2]

The student will benefit, largely, by extending his reading to the history of the dramatist's reception, through his works, on the Continent, and for this purpose the following will be found of great service :

Shakespeare in Germany in the 16th and 17th Centuries: an Account of English Actors in Germany, &c. by Albert Cohn. 1865. *How Shakespeare became Popular in Germany,* by Eleanor Marx. (In *The Gentleman's Magazine* for June, 1880), and *Shakespeare in France,* by Dr. John Doran (*Vide, The Nineteenth Century,* in LIST OF SELECTED ARTICLES, sub. 1878. May.)

---

[2] As most of these works are not easily obtainable, the reader will find this subject fully dealt with in, *The Era,* July 1st, 1877. Art: "The Mysteries and Moralities of the Early English Stage."

The quarrels of Shakespearean critics occupy now-a-days rather a conspicuous place in our periodical and pamphlet literature, which occasionally burst into volcanic fury; signally, the apparently never-ceasing feud between Mr. F. J. Furnivall and Mr. A. C. Swinburne; which has the mastery of invective and incisiveness of style, may be easily determined by him who will run and read; in their place will be found some references to the letters of these Shakespeareans, to which is added, in the LIST OF WORKS, under 1876 (merely to complete this curious and diverting literature), the extraordinary pamphlet entitled *Furnivallos Furioso.* Anyone calmly and dispassionately reading it, will at once sympathise with the scholar attacked, whose humility and kindness to those from whom he may differ, are universally recognised: and whose services rendered to the cause of Shakespearean study are invaluable. Ever ready to respect the views of others, he is always anxious to avoid all forms of personality in the discussion of topics concerning the works of the poet. Egotism will not be found on his side in the various disputes, and pity it is that literary discussions cannot be conducted in the same high spirit on the other side. Modesty was taught to be a virtue by the great luminary, and the right to one's opinion upon metrical or other tests has not, and can never be, usurped. The pamphlet, however, may be read without the appreciation of Shakespeare being in any way endangered, or his fame lessened.

Added hereto are a few *Notes on Shakespeare,* which the writer has had struck off the stereotype plate of a *brochure,* presented to the *Urban Club* on the occasion of their Shakespearean Festival, held on the 24th of April, 1876, under the presidency of the late esteemed and accomplished scholar, Dr. John Doran, and which has been incorporated in *Notes on Shakespeare, and Memorials of the Urban Club,* London, 1876, and in the privately printed enlarged edition of 1877.

J. JEREMIAH.

KESWICK HOUSE,
QUADRANT ROAD, CANONBURY, N.,
June 20th, 1880.

Hand List of Works and Articles,

(WITH CONDENSED NOTES,) COMPILED AS

AN AID TO SHAKESPEAREAN STUDY.

(SELECTED FROM MY LIBRARY.)

I.—LIST OF WORKS. [1]

Those marked with an asterisk (*) can be recommended to the beginner in the Study of the Dramatist and his Works. Many other valuable Works, than those mentioned, will suggest themselves to the general reader.

The sign † indicates those Works that have become very scarce and not easily procurable.

The sign ‖ are Privately Printed Works, and are not obtainable through the ordinary channels.

DATE.

1623. *The First Folio. Fac-simile Reprint, by J. O. Halliwell-Phillipps, F.R.S., 1876. *(Indispensable to the student.)*

1623 (?). †A Tragi-Coomodie. Called The Witch, by T. Middleton. Reprinted by J. Nicholls, 1778. (Interesting in regard to *Macbeth*.)

1691. *†An Account of the English Dramatick Poets, by Gerald Langbaine.

1726. †A Compleat Catalogue of All the Plays, &c. Printed for W. Mears.
(Founded upon Langbaine).

1767. *An Essay on the Learning of Shakespeare, by R. Farmer, B.D. (2nd ed.)
(On the question of Shakespeare's alleged Classical Learning.)

1774. *A Philosophical Analysis, &c. of some of Shakespeare's Remarkable Characters, by W. Richardson.
(Treats of Macbeth, Hamlet, Jacques, and Imogen, with moralisings.)

1778. †The Fashionable Tell-Tale. Dedicated to David Garrick, Esq.
(For spurious Shakespearean anecdotes).

1781. *†The History of English Poetry, by Thomas Warton, B.D. (1st Edition, 3 Vols.)[2]
(In Vol. 3, an account of the general character of the Elizabethan poets.)

1783. *Remarks, &c. on the Facts and Notes of the last Edition of Shakespeare, by J. Ritson.
(Contains many reasonable emendations. Attacks Steevens' Notes in his edition.)

1796. *An Inquiry into the Authenticity of Certain Papers, &c., by E. Malone.
(An *exposé* of the Ireland Forgeries.)

---

[1] Quarterly Reviews are classified as *Works*.

[2] Later editions of this valuable work, may be consulted, especially the one in 4 vols. by W. C. Hazlitt. Ritson's edition is too full of valueless ascerbities, and mar that editor's scholarship.

1797. †Macbeth: A Tragedy, &c., with Notes by Harry Rowe.
(For some novel emendations).

1799. †Vortigern: An Historical Play, &c., by W. H. Ireland.
With an original Preface, &c. 1832. (A Shakespeare fabrication.) [3]
(The most celebrated of the Ireland Forgeries.)

1801. *†Barker's Continuation of Egerton's Theat: Remembrancer,
etc. by W. C. Oulton. [4]
(A Catalogue of Plays.)

1807. *Comments on the Commentators on Shakespeare, by H. J. Pye.
(An uncompromising attack upon, and exposé of, the vagaries of Steevens,
Johnson, Malone, Ritson, &c. in textual emendations; in some
instances deserved. (Gives some curious counter emendations of the
text.)

„ *Observations on the Fairy Queen of Spenser, by Thomas
Warton, A.M. A new edition (2 vols.)
(In vol. 1, p. 179 will be found portions of the Ballad of *Gernutus, the
Jew of Venice,* with remarks thereon. He suggests that Shakespeare
copied from this ballad, and altered *Gernutus* to *Shylock*.)[5]

1809. †The Theatrical Banquet, &c., by W. Oxberry (2 vols.)
(For anecdotes of Shakespearean Actors.)

1811. †A Tour in Quest of Genealogy, &c., by a Barrister (by
Fenton of Bristol).
(Containing Shakespeare fabrications.)

1823. *†King Henry VIII, &c. with Prefatory Remarks by W.
Oxberry, Comedian.
(Gives the Stage history of *Henry VIII* and *The Winter's Tale.*)

„ *Ancient Mysteries Described, &c., by William Hone.
(Contains a long chapter on "Hearne's Print of the Descent into Hell,"
and reviews the various meanings suggested, of Shakespeare's use
of the words "*Aroint* thee, witch!" *Macbeth* Act 1, s. 3, and "And
aroynt thee, witch, aroynt thee!" *King Lear* Act iii, s. 5. Hone
suggests, aroint,—aroynt,—arougt,—a summons to assemble. *Vide*
p.p. 138-147).

1824. *Reliques of Ancient English Poetry, by Bishop Percy.
(4 vols., 6th ed.) [6]
(See chapter on the Origin of Stage).

[No Date] Fairy Legends and Traditions of the South of Ireland, by
T. Crofton Croker, Esq A new and completed edition
edited by T. Wright, Esq., M.A., &c., with a Memoir by
his son T. F. Dillon Croker, Esq., F.S.A.
(For a remark at p. 201 on the Commentators on Shakespeare, deriving
the Puck of the *Midsummer Night's Dream,* from the Pouk or Phooka,
from which the author appears to differ).

1833. *The Fairy Mythology, by T. Keightley. (2 Vols.)
(In Vol. 2, an account of the Fairy-lore of Shakespeare, page 118, *et seq.)*

---

[3] An immense amount of literature upon the Ireland Controversy, issued from
the press in the last century: the most amusing however of the satires is entitled,
"Passages selected by Distinguished Personages of the great literary Trial of
Vortigern and Rowena, a Comi-Tragedy," by Sir Pato Dudley and his lady. 1795-8,
in 4 volumes.

[4] Mr. J. O. Halliwell's work *A Dictionary of Old Plays,* will be of invaluable
service for Plays of the Shakespearean period.

[5] This Ballad is given in *extenso* in Percy's "Reliques of Ancient English
Poetry," 6th edition 1844, vol 2. pp. 15-22.

[6] Other editions also contain this interesting chapter.

1840. *Kemp's Nine Daies' Wonder, edited, &c., by the Rev. A. Dyce. (Camden Soc. Pub.)
(Introduction contains an account of Kemp, and the parts he acted in Shakespeare's plays. An actor in the Chamberlain's Company.) (Shakespeare's.) [7]

„ *The Quarterly Review. March. Art: Hunter on Shakespeare's Tempest.
(Strongly attacks the theorisings of the Rev. J. Hunter.)

„ "On Heroes, Hero-Worship and The Heroic in History," by T. Carlyle.
(A finely written estimate of Shakespeare, but strangely enough, he accepts the unfounded deer-stalking incident. He says, "had the Warwickshire Squire not prosecuted him for deer-stalking, we had perhaps never heard of him as a poet." Page 94. Edition 1872.)

1841. *†On the Character of Sir John Falstaff, &c., by J. O. Halliwell, F.R.S.
(Opposes the idea that the characters of Fastolf and Falstaff have any connection with each other.)

1846. *A course of Lectures on Dramatic Art and Literature, by A. W. Schlegel (translated by John Black.)
(For Æsthetic criticism of Shakespeare's plays.)

1849. *Studies on Shakspere, by Charles Knight.

„ *The Æsthetic and Miscellaneous Works of F. von Schlegel; (translated by E. J. Millington.)
(Vide remarks on Shakespeare. To be read with great caution.)

„ The Quarterly Review. September. pp. 357 et seq.
(Shakespeare's description of the deaths of Falstaff, Cordelia, &c.)

„ *Observations on the Popular Antiquities of Great Britain, by J. Brand, M.A. Revised &c., by Sir Henry Ellis, K.H., F.R.S., &c. (3 vols.)
(For remarks in passim, upon the Fairy Mythology of Shakespeare, in vol. 2, p. 494 et seq.) [8]

1851. †An Essay upon the Ghost-Belief of Shakespeare, by Alfred Roffe.
(Endeavours to prove Shakespeare's belief in Ghosts).

„ *The Works of William Shakespeare, edited by Samuel Phelps, (2 vols).
(Although this work is stated to be edited by Mr. S. Phelps—the actor—yet such was not the case. His name was used, but the work was done by Mr. E. L. Blanchard, the well-known dramatist and author. It contains a most interesting account of the Life and Times of Shakespeare, and is interspersed with many valuable Notes to the text)

1853. *Curiosities of Modern Criticism, by J. O. Halliwell, F.R.S.
(A reply to a rancorous attack upon this author's Folio Edition of the Works of Shakespeare, which appeared in the Athenæum.)

1855. Songs from the Dramatists, edited by Robert Bell.
(Contains the Songs and Snatches of old Ballads in Shakespeare's Works, with a few notes on some of them).

„ *On Celtic Words used by early English Writers, by the Rev. John Davies, M.A.
(Ascribes to Celtic sources, some words used by Shakespeare, id. est.: grise, grize; imp: braid; coddis-garter; bollen; esil, eysell; brach: latch'd; safe; pick; coystrel; and puttock. Many of the derivations are ingenious and well deserve the attention of the student). [9]

[7] For particulars of Kemp's Continental journeyings, vide. Ludus Coventriæ. [The Coventry Mysteries], edited by J. O. Halliwell, F.R.S., 1841, pp. 409-10. Old Shakespeare Society's Publication.
[8] This work has been re-edited, and published in 4 vols. by W.C. Hazlitt, and in many respects is to be preferred.
[9] This is a reprint from the Cambrian Journal, vol. II.

---

[1] To those desirous of further studying the COLLIER AND PERKINS' FOLIO CONTROVERSY, the following works are recommended:- A COMPLETE VIEW OF THE SHAKESPEARE CONTROVERSY, by Dr. C. M. Ingleby, M.A., 1861; A REVIEW OF THE PRESENT STATE OF THE SHAKESPEARIAN CONTROVERSY, by T. Duffus Hardy, 1860; and AN INQUIRY INTO THE GENUINENESS OF THE MANUSCRIPT CORRECTIONS IN COLLIER'S ANNOTATED SHAKESPEARE, FOLIO 1632, by N. E. S. A. Hamilton, 1860. (Dr. Ingleby's A COMPLETE VIEW, &c. also contains a critical examination and *exposé* of the Devonshire, Ellesmere, Dulwich, and State Paper Office, Forgeries.)

1864. *The London Quarterly Review. *April.* Article: "Shakespeare."
(Contains Goethe's estimate of Shakespeare's genius; and prefers Schiller for pure *force of imagination*; Scott for a superior *creative genius*; and Byron for *superiority of description*, as for example, his Seige of Ismail in *Don Juan.*)

1865. *Shakespeare's Library, ed. by W. C. Hazlitt. 6 vols.
(For sources of Shakespeare's Plays.)

1866. *Six old English Chronicles, &c. (Translated). Edited with illustrative Notes, by J. A. Giles, D.C.L.
(For the Story of Leir (Lear) and his three daughters, Gonorilla, Regan, and Cordelia, as given by *Geoffrey of Monmouth*, also that of Kymbelinus (Cymbeline).)

" " Chronicum Scotorum. A Chronicle of Irish Affairs," &c., translated and edited by W. M. Hennessy, M.R.I.A, (*Rolls Publication.*)
(For Irish account of death of Macbeth, p. 285.)

1867. *The "Globe" Edition of Shakespeare's Works, by W. G. Clark and W. Aldis Wright.

1868. *The Four Ancient Books of Wales, &c., by W. F. Skene (2 vols.)
(For original story of King Lear (or Llyr) and his Children.)

1869. *Six Doubtful Plays of William Shakespeare, (*Tauchnitz* edition. Leipzig.)
(Contains Edward III. Thomas Lord Cromwell. Locrine. A Yorkshire Tragedy. The London Prodigal. The Birth of Merlin.)

" *Characters of Shakespeare's Plays, by W. Hazlitt. (Reprint)

1870. *Lectures on The Literature of the Age of Elizabeth, &c., by W. Hazlitt. (Reprint).

" *The Tempest, with Bibliographical Preface, &c., by the Rev. J. Hunter, M.A. (Also the Series of the Plays.)

" *Notes and Conjectural Emendations of Certain Doubtful Passages in Shakespeare's Plays, by P. A. Daniel.

" Hamlet; from a Psychological Point of View, by W. Dyson Wood.
(The writer says:—" I prefer to regard him myself as a splendid specimen of humanity, full of promise, but arrested in his developement, and that too in the very blossoming of his powers.")

1872. *Clubs and Club Life in London, by John Timbs, F.S.A. (For an interesting account of the *Mermaid* and *Boar's Head* Taverns).

1873. *A new Variorum Edition of Shakespeare, by H. H. Furness,
    *1873. Romeo and Juliet .... 1 vol. ⎫
    * "   Macbeth .... 1 vol. ⎬ 2
    *1877. Hamlet .... 2 vols. ⎭
    *1880. King Lear .... 1 vol.
(Each volume contains the views and comments of all the commentators upon the respective plays.)

" *The Orkneyinga Saga (Translated.) Edited with Notes and Introduction, by J. Anderson.
(For History of Magblod, suggestive of *Macbeth*.)

1874. *A Concordance to Shakespeare's Poems (1 vol.) by Mrs. Horace Howard Furness.

---

2 These volumes contain an almost complete Bibliography of Shakespeare. Every Student should have them.

1874. *†Illustrations of the Life of Shakespeare, by J. O. Halliwell-Phillipps, F.R.S. Part I. [3]
(Contains many valuable facts regarding the Life, and the Poet's connection with Burbage).

„ *The Philosophy of Hamlet, by T. Tyler, M.A.
(Tries to prove it was Pessimistic.)

„ *The Still Lion, &c., by C. M. Ingleby, M.A., L.L.D.
(For criticism of emendations, &c.)

„ *The Succession of Shakspere's Works, &c., by F. J. Furnivall, M.A.
(Being the Introduction to the English translation of Gervinus's Commentaries on Shakespeare [by Miss Bunnett].)

„ *Shakespeare's Centurie of Prayse, by C. M. Ingleby, M.A., L.L.D.
(Early allusions to the Poet and his Works.)

„ *Shakspere Allusion-Books. Part I, by C. M. Ingleby, M.A., L.L.D. (New Shakspere Society.)
(Based upon *The Centurie of Prayse*, so far as it went. The *Allusions* are printed in *extenso*).

„ ●Prospectus of the New Shakspere Society," by F. J. Furnivall, M.A.
(For Metrical Tests.)

1875. *Shakespeare's Plutarch. (For Origin, &c., of Shakespeare's Plays,) edited by the Rev. Walter W. Skeat, M.A.

„ *Fairy Tales, &c. Illustrating Shakespeare's Fairy-lore, &c. Ed. by W. C. Hazlitt.

„ *A History of Eng: Dram: Literature, by A. W. Ward, M.A. (2 vols.)
(Of general value.)

„ Shakespeare's King Edward the Third. An Indignation Pamphlet, by A. Teetgen.
(Very curious, maintains Shakespeare's sole authorship.)

[No date] *Shakspeare's Sonnets, edited by the Rev. A. Dyce.
(With an interesting Memoir of the Poet.) *(Aldine Poets.)*

„ "Representative Actors," by W. Clarke Russell.
(A chatty and interesting account of the Elizabethan and later Actors. Contains a concise " Notice on English Acting.")

1876. *Shakspeare's Dramatic Art, by D. H. Ulrici (2 vols.)
(Translated by L. Dora Schmitz).

„ *Shakespeare Manual, by F. G. Fleay, M.A. [4]
(Fairly good, contains much about Metrical Tests, to be read with reservation.)

„ *A Study of Shakespeare's Portraits, by W. Page.
(On restoration of his Portrait. Believes in the genuineness of the Becker or Kesselstadt death-mask, of the poet.)

„ *Celtic Scotland. A History of Ancient Alban, by W. F. Skene. (2 vols. *In progress*).
(For History of Macbeth in vol. 1. p. 405.)

---

[3] This work is complete in itself; and no other volume will be published. It contains many valuable facts.

[4] Of this work, Professor Dowden says it "may be found useful, if read with care, to distinguish the writer's theories from ascertained facts." *Shakspere* (Lit. Primer), p. 167

1876. *A Short History of the English People, by J. R. Green, M.A.
(For a well-considered and admirable account of the Elizabethan Poets, especially of Shakespeare.)

,, English Literature, (*Literature Primer*) by the Rev. Stopford Brooke, M.A. (3rd edition).[5]
(Gives in the small space of six pages [pp. 83-88] a very clear account of the poet's works. It also contains a very concise account of the English Drama, especially of the Elizabethan Period; and not rendered difficult and confusing to the beginner, by *Metrical* and *Æsthetic* Tests.)

,, Furnivallos Furioso! and The Newest Shakespeare Society. A Dram-attic Squib of the Period. In Three Fizzes. And let off for the occasion by the Ghost of Guido Fawkes.
(Has been *ascribed* to Mr. Swinburne. Some have considered this amusing little book, complimentary to Mr. Furnivall, but others do not.)

,, Sheridan Knowles' Conception and Mr. Irving's Perform- ance of Macbeth. (*Anon.*)
(Draws a comparison between Sheridan Knowles' view and Mr. Irving acting of the character, and objects to that of the latter. Says:— "But the radical defect of his conception of Macbeth's character at the outset—a conception which tends to transform Shakespeare's great play into melodrama, ... gives a want of truth of harmony and consistency to Mr. Irving's performance as a whole.")

1877. *Shakspere, (*Literature Primer*) by E. Dowden, L.L.D.
(A condensed account of the life and works of the Poet.)

,, *Shakespeare. The Man and the Book, by C. M. Ingleby, M.A., L.L.D. (Part the First). [6]
(Containing some valuable papers on the Bard and his writings including a critical examination of the Bacon Controversy.)

,, *The Mabinogion. From the Welsh of the "Llyfr Coch O Hergest." Translated with Notes, by Lady Charlotte Guest. (New edition).
(For the stories of Branwen and Manawyddan, children of King Llyr [or Lear].)

,, *Shakespeare's King Richard III. Arranged for the Stage, by H. Irving. [7]

,, Remarks on Shakespeare, His Birth-place, &c., by C. Roach Smith.
(A general account of some Shakespeare traditions, and his birth-place).

,, *Gesta Romanorum. Translated by the Rev. Charles Swan; revised, &c., by Wynnard Hooper, B.A.
(For Originals of Merchant of Venice, King Lear, and Pericles.)

,, *Ancient Songs and Ballads, collected by Joseph Ritson, Esq. 3rd Edition; by W. Carew Hazlitt.
(Contains a "Dissertation on Ancient Songs and Music," with some valuable notes on the Songs and Ballads used by Shakespeare.)

[No date] *Nursery Rhymes and Nursery Tales of England, by James Orchard Halliwell. 5th Edition.
(Most valuable for the Nursery-lore of Shakespeare).

---

5 This author's more recent and enlarged edition 1880, is to be preferred.
6 Part II. in the Press. This volume will complete this work, and will contain essays on *The Tongue of Sh.; Tests of Authorship; Metrical Tests, as applied by Mr. Fleay; The Hamlet of 1603; Conjectural Criticism applied to Sh.; The Literary Forgeries of Ireland;* etc.
7 Here mentioned for comparison of text and punctuation, with the "Globe" Edition of Shakespeare's Works, and the *First Folio*, 1623.

1877. *Introduction to Shakespearian Study, by Rev. F. G. Fleay, M.A. (*Collins' School and College Classics.*)
(A most useful account of the dramatist and his works; not so weighted as this author's *Shakespeare Manual*, 1876, with metrical conjectures and calculations. The concluding chapter is however concerned with æsthetic conjectures and ought to be read with caution.)

1877-9. *Prof. Wilson on "Time Analysis of Macbeth and Othello," Edited by Dr. C. M. Ingleby, M.A.
(New Shakspere Society Publication).

,, *N. J. Halpin on "Time Analysis of The Merchant of Venice." Edited by Dr. C. M. Ingleby, M.A.
(New Shakspere Society Publication.)

,, *Shakespeare. Select Plays, ed. by W. Aldis Wright, M.A. (Clarendon Press. *In progress*).
(Plays issued:—The Tempest; As You Like It; Julius Cæsar; King Lear; A Midsummer Night's Dream; Coriolanus; The Merchant of Venice; Richard the Second; Macbeth.) (*Separate vols.*)

,, *P. A. Daniel on "Time Analysis of the Plots of Shakespeare's Plays" (Series I, Part II). (New Shakspere Society Publication.) This Volume also contains a paper by T. A. Spedding, on "The First Quarto of Romeo and Juliet." Is there any evidence of a second hand?

,, A History of the Shakespeare Memorial, Stratford-on-Avon. Published for the Council of the Shakespeare Memorial Association.

1878. *A Shakespearian Grammar, by E. A. Abbott, D.D.

,, *An Attempt to determine the Chron: Order of Shakespeare's Plays, by the Rev. H. P. Stokes, B.A.
(Largely weighted with the Metrical and Æsthetic modes of treatment, but on the whole a very useful work.)

,, Studies of the Text of Shakespeare, by J. Bulloch.
(Textual emendations).

,, *The School of Shakspere, by R. Simpson, B.A. (2 vols.)
(For the Plays that were acted by the Lord Chamberlaine's Company.)

,, *The "Leopold" Shakspere, by F. J. Furnivall. (For "Introduction"). (Text after Prof. Delius.)

,, *Old Southwark and its People, by W. Rendle, F.R.C.S.
(For numerous particulars concerning the history of Sir John Fastolf. He says: "Well, I do not say that Falstaff was Fastolf; that I cannot quite do. Falstaff was very much a caricature or invention of the poet for stage purposes." Page 62).

,, *Southwark in the time of Shakspere. The Bankside—Theatres, Stews, &c., by W. Rendle, F.R.C.S.
(Contains an historical account of the Theatres in Southwark, including the *Globe*, and its site. A most important work, and the facts accurately stated.)

,, Fairy Tales. Their Origin and Meaning, by J. T. Bunce.
(Contains a short account of fairy-lore in reference to Shakespeare's *Midsummer Night's Dream, and The Merry Wives of Windsor.*)

,, The Speeches of George Dawson on Shakespeare, including two Lectures on Hamlet. Selected by C. C. Cattell.
(Very interesting and instructive.)

1878. *The Encyclopœdia Britannica, (9th edition, *in progress.*) Art: "Celtic Literature," by W. K. Sullivan.

(For concise account of the Celtic Legends of Queen Mebh (Mab) and Llyr, Lir, or Lear, which formed the groundwork of Shakespeare's Midsummer Night's Dream and King Lear. The art: "Drama" is on the whole a valuable contribution.)

1879. ‖Memoranda on the Midsummer Night's Dream, by J. O. Halliwell-Phillipps, F.R.S. [8]

(The writer says: "There is no good evidence that the Midsummer Night's Dream was written any length of time before the month of September, 1598, at which period it is mentioned by Meres under the title of "*Midsummer's night Dreame.*" "The accounts of the bad weather of 1594 are valueless in the question of chronology." He is opposed to the gratuitous and silly conjectures of Elze, Kurz, and Dowden, that it was written to do honour to the marriage of the Earl of Essex, in 1590, as stated by Mr. Stokes in his "Attempt to Determine the Chronological Order of Shakespeare's Plays," p. 48; also to the application of "what is absurdly termed æsthetic criticism," in analysing this play.)

„ ‖Memoranda on the Tragedy of Hamlet, by J. O. Halliwell-Phillipps, F.R.S. [8]

(In his preface, the writer remarks—and every student should well consider the sentence—"That the more I read of the tragedy of Hamlet, the less I really understand it as a whole, and now despair of meeting with any theories that will reconcile its perplexing inconsistencies, making, of course, allowances for those that are most likely intentional." He is opposed to Goethe's opinion "that in Hamlet the great dramatist intended to delineate an irresolute mind oppressed by the weight of a mission which it is unable to accomplish," pp. 13-14. Hamlet "is really a man of singular determination, and, excepting in occasional paroxysms, one of powerful self-control." "Much of the difficulty in the interpretation of the tragedy arises from the oversight of accepting his soliloquies as continuous illustrations of his character, instead of being, as they mostly are, transient emanations of his subtle irritability." "A wide distinction also must be drawn in the matter of time for vengeance. between action resulting from sudden, and that from remoter, provocation." He then gives the "earliest allusions to the *old* tragedy of Hamlet, from Nash in his edition of Green's *Menaphon*, 1589, and one that occurs in Lodge's *Wits Miserie*, 1596, which refer to a pre-Shakesperean drama, and was played at Newington, as recorded in Henslowe's Diary, in 1594, by "my Lord Admeralle and my lorde Chamberlen men." "As Shakespeare was a member of the Lord Chamberlain's Company at that time, it is certain that he must have been well acquainted with the older play of Hamlet," p. 19. After giving a very lucid account of the various editions of Hamlet, and the early mode of representing the play on the stage, he concludes this most masterly essay with some very sensible and timely remarks upon the futility of Æsthetic Criticism, and says "For my own part I believe that æsthetic or as Mr. Aldis Wright felicitously terms it, sign-post criticism, unless restricted within the narrowest practical limits, is positively mischevious. . . . . and it is, moreover, my present firm belief that no two characters in Shakespeare are either identical or the germ one of the other, that each play was written by itself and for itself without any design of consonance with the others and that it should be so read; but at the same time, it is hardly necessary to say that a longer course of study may modify these views. Those who have lived as long as myself in the midst of Shakesperean Criticism will be careful not to be too certain of anything," pp. 77-78.)

„ ‖Which shall it be, &c.—Shaxpere or Shakespeare? by J. O. Halliwell-Phillipps, F.R.S. [8]

(Advocates the long spelling of the name. Says "that he ought to be known now in literature, as Shakespeare is sufficiently established by the testimony of Ben Jonson and many others.")

---

[8] All these Works are *privately printed.*

1879. ‖Memoranda on All's Well that End's Well, The Two Gentlemen of Verona, Much ado about Nothing, and Titus Andronicus, by J. O. Halliwell-Phillipps, F.R.S. ᵇ

(Gives source of the serious portion of ALL'S WELL THAT ENDS WELL, from William Painter's PALACE OF PLEASURE, 1566, reprinted 1575, being a translation of the story related by Boccaccio in his DECAMERON, ninth novel of the third day. Inclines to the opinion that the original title of this play was "LOVE'S LABOUR'S WON," which, if correct, removes the date from 1623 to 1598 in which year Mere's mentions the latter title in his PALLADIS TAMIA. Upon THE TWO GENTLEMEN OF VERONA, Mr. Halliwell-Phillipps, says:— "As a rule it is unsafe to pronounce a judgment on the period of the composition of any of Shakespeare's dramas from internal evidence, but the general opinion that this play is one of the author's earliest complete dramatic efforts may be followed without much risk of error." Regarding the origin of the comedy, he says:— "There are a sufficient number of incidents and minute particulars common to the tale above analysed, [the tale of FELIX AND FELISMENA, written in Spanish by George of Montemayor, *circa* 16th century] and to Shakespeare's comedy to show that the plot of the latter was derived either from Montemayor, or from some other work, possibly the old English play just named, [THE HISTORY OF FELIX AND PHILIOMENA, acted before Queen Elizabeth in 1585,] in which use had been made of the tale of Felismena." The next play treated of in this book is MUCH ADO ABOUT NOTHING, the origin of the "serious portion of its plot, is derived from one of Bandello's novels, first published in the year 1554, which was probably known to Shakespeare in the French translation of Belleforest." "As far as our researches have yet extended, the probabilities are in favour of Shakespeare having either been indebted to Bandello, through the medium of Belleforest, or to some early English translation of the Italian novel, which may have been published in the sixteenth century, although no copy or fragment of such a work has yet been discovered."

TITUS ANDRONICUS. After a minute examination of this play and the history of its stage career, the author thus concludes:—"On reading TITUS ANDRONICUS once more, I trust for the last time, the Clown's speeches appear to me to be as much in his manner as any others, and that in them, if with certainty anywhere may be traced some of the few 'master touches,' if Ravenscroft's edition is to be accepted;⁹ but I do not really believe that Shakespeare wrote a single word of it."

This volume concludes with some brief remarks upon Shakespeare's name, which are incorporated in his "WHICH SHALL IT BE? &c.")

„ ‖Memoranda on Love's Labour's Lost, King John, Othello, and on Romeo and Juliet, by J. O. Halliwell-Phillipps, F.R.S. ᵇ

(LOVE'S LABOUR'S LOST. "The exact date at which the comedy was written will perhaps never be ascertained. The question is rendered exceedingly intricate by the probability that it received additions from its author shortly before the year 1598 . . . . The year 1597, as the date of the composition of the amended drama, agrees very well with all the external and internal evidences at present accessible." The main incidents of the play may have been taken "from some old romantic story not yet discovered." The author *does not agree* with some critics who maintain that, in the character of Holofernes, Shakespeare intended to satirize John Florio, and there is a strong probability that they were friends and not enemies. After a long account of the *Dancing Horse*, alluded to by Shakespeare, and additional notes on this comedy, the play of *King John* is commented upon. He alludes to Bishop Bale's play of *Kynge Johan*, and describes its plot and characters. He says of *King John* that "Shakespeare, following the custom adopted by his professional contemporaries, having constructed an abridged drama out of the

---

ᵇ All these Works are *privately printed*.

⁹ Ravenscroft published an alteration of his play in 1687. He says in the preface as cited by Mr. Halliwell-Phillipps :—"I have been told by some anciently conversant with the stage that it was not originally his, but brought out by a private author to be acted, and he only gave some master touches to one or two of the principal parts or characters."

materials afforded by this inferior old play, [THE TROUBLESOME RAIGNE OF IOHN, KING OF ENGLAND, 1591] but making, as usual, the subject so entirely his own as to preclude the suggestion of plagiarism in the objectionable sense of the term." The attribution of the authorship of the old play to William Rowley, Mr. Halliwell-Phillipps does not assent to. He says *King John* must have appeared before 1598, as it is mentioned by Meres in his *Palladis Tamia.* In the brief note on *Othello,* the author cites from the twelfth Public Act of the first Parliament of James the First (passed between March 19th and July 7th, 1604) which was levelled " against conjuration, witchcrafte and dealings with evill and wicked spirits;" in order to account for the form given to a part of the first act of Othello, where the Duke "tells Brabantio that his accusation of the employment of witchcraft shall be impartially investigated." (vide *act* i, *s.* III.) This Volume concludes with a Note on *Romeo and Juliet,* which contains the interesting statement that Simon Catling, referred to in that Play, was a real personage and in all probability known to the poet. He resided in Southwark. " The notion that the allusion to this play, in Weever's Epigrammes, is any evidence of its existence before the publication of that work in 1599, will not bear the test of examination.")

1879.   Shakespeare and his Contemporaries, &c. by W. Tegg.
        (Of no value and very inaccurate).

  ,,   *Scattered Notes on the Text of Shakespeare, by J. G. Herr. (Philadelphia). (Some curious emendations, &c.)

  ,. ||Mr. Swinburne's "Flat Burglary" on Shakspere, by F. J. Furnivall. [8] (A fierce attack upon Mr. A. C. Swinburne, of no value).

  ,,   *"Early Chroniclers of England." " England," by James Gairdner.
        (A concise account of Geoffrey of Monmouth's *History of the Kings of Britain,* also of *Hall* and *Hollingshead's Chronicles,* from which Shakespeare derived the materials of his dramatised Histories.)

  ,,   *Hamlet. First Quarto, 1603, facsimile (Photo-litho.), by W. Griggs. Introduction by F. J. Furnivall.
        (*Series in Progress*).

  ,,   "Old Celtic Romances." Translated from the Gaelic, by P. W. Joyce, L.L.D., &c.
        (For *Gaelic version* of the Romance of the Fate of the Children of Lir).

1880.   *A Study of Shakespeare, by A. C. Swinburne.
        (A well-considered and important contribution.)

  ,,   *School Lectures on the Electra of Sophocles and Macbeth, by A. H. Gilkes.
        (The Lectures on *Macbeth* give in a very succinct manner, the plot, and and an analysis of the various characters of the play.)

  ,, ||New Lamps or Old, &c. ? Respecting the E and the A, by J. O. Halliwell-Phillipps, F.R.S. [b]
        (On the spelling of Shakespeare's name—maintains the full spelling viz., Shakespeare.)
        (A re-examination of the question of the spelling of the poet's name. Most students will probably consider the following passages as finally settling this problem:—" A distinguished scholar," says the author, "has just pointed out to me—and it is, as, in the case of the management of the egg by Columbus, most singularly curious so obvious a fact should have escaped the notice of all others— that the character following the letter *k* is the then well-known and accepted contraction for *es* [1] There cannot be a doubt on this point, and therefore the poet's last signature appears in his own selected literary form of Shakespeare.")

  ,,   *" British Goblins, Welsh Folk-lore, &c.," by Wirt Sikes.
        (For Shakespeare's use of Welsh folk-lore, and origin of his Queen *Mab.,* in *Romeo and Juliet* and Titania, in *Midsummer Night's Dream*.)

  ,,   *Teutonic Mythology, by Jacob Grimm; translated by James Steven Stallybrass. Vol. I. (*In progress.*)
        (For Origin of the *Weird Sisters,* Macbeth, Chap. *Norni,* p. 407).

---

[8] All these Works are *privately printed.*
[1] *Vide* Fac-similes of the signatures.

SELECTED ARTICLES, &c.

IN

MONTHLY MAGAZINES AND PERIODICALS.

1871. April 1. Review of a book entitled "Was Shakespeare a Lawyer," &c., by H—— T——.
(Rightly ridicules the nonsense of this anonymous compiler.)

,, June 10. "The Earliest Notice of Shakspeare as a Poet," by J. McGarth.
(Shows that Mr. Scott's discovery of a MS. tract on "The Excellency of the English Tongue," which is said to contain "undoubtedly an earlier notice of Shakspeare as a poet than any mentioned by his biographers" (referred to in this paper of the 27th May), has been anticipated by Malone in his Notes to *Venus and Adonis.*)

,, Oct. 28. *"On The Phyrrus and Hecuba in Hamlet," by R. G. Latham.
(Shakespeare's indebtedness to an old play for these characters, &c.)

1872. Mar. 16. "Euripides and Shakspeare," by F. Cunningham.
(Referring to Dr. Latham's letter of the 28th October, 1871, says he gives conclusive reasons for "supposing that Shakspeare must have been acquainted with the ' Hecuba ' of Euripides," and says further, that Charles Fox had the same conviction with regard to another play, the ' Alcestis.')

,, July 27. "On Fortinbras as a Name; and on the Two Bearers of it in Shakespeare's ' Hamlet,' " by R.G.L.
(The etymological hypothesis of this writer is, that the name translated, (after dwelling upon its French forms,) into Icelandic and English, becomes *Jarnsidhe* and *Ironside*.)

,, Nov. 2. *"Unsuspected Corruptions of Shakespeare's Text" by H. Staunton.
(Continued through various numbers to June 27, 1874—very valuable contributions).

1873. April 12. *"On Wappened Widow," in Timon of Athens, by M. C.[2]
(On Shadwell's plagiary, in his *Timon of Athens, the Man Hater,* altered passage to "warped and withered widows.")

,, May 24. *"On Woe-pin'd for Wappened Widow," in ditto, by F. J. Furnivall.

,, June 21. "Cymbeline, *Act IV.*, *sec. 2*," by F. J. Furnivall.
(Answers Mr. Staunton's query, "What can be meant by ' find the ooze ? ' " and says " Why, just find the ooze to be sure." . . . . "It is not necessary to suppose the actual settling in soft mud, as Shakespeare uses only the words ' easiliest harbour in.' ")

,, July 12. "A Shakespeare Study," by W. L. R. Cates.
(On "*Race* of Night;" King John, Act III, s. 3, line 39. Suggesting restoration of "race" as in First Folio, and means "swiftness," *e.g.* "race." in names of rivers, and sea currents, a familiar example, Race of Alderney, and Teign Race in South Devon, &c.)

,, Oct. 25. "A Shakespearean Discovery," by C. Edmonds.
(Announces his discovery of an "unique copy of a poem, apparently unknown, written by the well-known Robert Southwell." *Vide* further discussion of this in the writer's letter of Nov. 22nd, same year.)

[2] Dr. C. M. Ingleby, in "The Englishman's Magazine" Nov. 1865. Suggests "Wappen'd"=hackneyed, p. 449.

1873. Nov. 22. *"On 'W.H.' query," in re Sonnets, by C. Edmonds.
(This writer is convinced " of the identity of the Shakespeare ' W.H.' with the ' W.H.' of Southwell's poem ; I agree with Chalmers who says ' W.H.' was the *bringer forth* of the Sonnets.")

1874. Jan. 31. *"Unsuspected Corruptions of Shakespeare's Text," by Howard Staunton.
(Treating of the Sonnets.)

,,　　Feb. 21. *"On the *Perkin's Folio of* 1632," by J. Payne Collier.
(Citing Dyce's estimate of its emendations.)

,,　　Mar. 28. "Shakspeare's ' Edward the Third,' " by J. Payne Collier.
(Enters upon his reasons for stating that this play is Shakespeare's.)

,,　　May 30. "The Taming of the Shrew," by F. G. Fleay.
(Merely a rejoinder to an attack made by Mr. Furnivall in the *Athenæum* of the 23rd May, 1874. *Neither of any value.*)

,,　　June 24. *"The Winter's Tale," Act 1, s. 2. A general estimate of this passage, and the Play, by Howard Staunton.

,,　　Sept. 19. "New Shakspere Society," by F. G. Fleay.
(A protest against the discourteous treatment of this writer, and says, " Had I listened to the warnings of my late friend, Mr. Staunton, I should have been spared this, but, unfortunately, I attributed his well-meant cautions to personal feeling, arising from his having been anticipated in carrying out his favorite idea, by one to whom he had himself communicated his intention." Surely the *scholar* here alluded to (whoever he may be), could not have been guilty of such a breach of confidence ?)

,,　　Sept. 19. "An Early Notice of Shakspeare," by G. Bullen.
(Directs attention to an early notice of the poet, which appears to have escaped observation, date 1651.)

,,　　Dec. 5. *"Timon of Athens," Act IV, s. 3, l. 38. On the meaning of the word *wop-eyed* (suggests *weep-eyed*), by W. W. Skeat.

1875. April 3. "Notes on Hamlet attributed to the Earl of Rochester," by C. Elliot Browne.
(Gives quotations from " The Poetical Works of that witty Lord John, Earl of Rochester, &c., 1761;" showing " corrections," &c., of Shakespeare's text.)

,,　　April 10. "Is *Aetion* Shakspeare ?" by F. G. Fleay.
(A long letter, in support of Todd's view that *Aetion* is Drayton.)

,,　　May 22. "Early allusions to Shakspeare," by C. Elliot Browne.
(Gives a few additional allusions, not mentioned in the first edition of Dr. Ingleby's " Centurie of Prayse.")

,,　　June 19. "The Meaning of Aetion," by J. W. Hales.
(To show that Mr. Fleay has been anticipated last year in a contemporary journal, by Mr. Minto.)

,,　　July 17. *"Shakespearean Imitations," by Prof. J. W. Hales
(On influence of Shakespeare over his contemporaries).

1876. Jan. 15. Strictures on F. G. Fleay, for an article entitled
" Who wrote 'Henry VI ?'" by A. C. Swinburne.

,, April 1. " Parallel Passages," by H. Schütz Wilson.
(Points out a passage in Mr. Munro's *Lucretius*, Book IV.,
948—989, upon *dreams*, and its parallel in *Mercutio's*
description of dreams, and *Queen Mab's* speech, to show
that the same idea forms the basis of the fancy; also
cites a passage from Mr. Fitzgerald's translation of
" Rubáiyát, of Omar Khayyám," containing the same
thought as Shakespeare's, upon the *undiscover'd
country*. Omar died in 1123.)

,, May 20. *"On Mucedorus." *Partly* by Shakespeare, by
J. Payne Collier.

,, Ditto by F. G. Fleay
(Protests against Mr. Collier's assertion.)

,, June 24. Ditto by J. Payne Collier.

,, July 29. *"Notes on Shakespeare's Names," by C. E. Elliot
Browne.
(On the names in "As You Like it," "Winter's Tale,"
"Hamlet," and "All's Well.")

,, Sept. 30. *" Notes on Shakespeare's Names." (Art. 3) by
C. Elliot Browne.
(On origin of the names of Shakespeare's characters.)

,, Oct. 7. *" What did Shakespeare learn at School?" by
F. J. Furnivall.
(Upon the books used in Grammar Schools, co-temporary
with that of Stratford-upon-Avon, and gives list of same.
Gives a list of probable School Books in use at the Stratford
Grammar School, about 1570.)

,, Oct. 14. *"The Story of Romeo and Juliet," by Alfred
Wallis.
(Gives the story, from an old and obscure work, " The
Treasurie of Auncient and Moderne Times," printed
by W. Iaggard, 1619.)

1877. Mar. 31. " Runawaye's Eyes," by Dr. Brinsley Nicholson.
(Suggests "lu-na's-eyes, (trisyllabic)—the moon's eyes, as
opposed to Mr. Collier's guess that it means *Cupid*.)

,, April 14. " The Court of Love," by A. C. Swinburne.
(An attack—and not very tender—on Mr. F. J. Furnivall
(and worth reading, even for amusement), and inciden-
tally, on his hypothesis regarding the authorship of
Pericles.)

,, April 21. Do., by F. J. Furnivall.
(Although not mainly on a Shakespearean topic, this
reference is given as closing this controversy; thus
the Editor—" We cannot print any more letters on
this subject." How strange! such acerbity and ill-
nature, and yet about *The Court of Love!*)

,, May 5. " Strictures on H. Irving's Notes on "Shakespeare," in the *Nineteenth Century*, by Moy
Thomas.

,, May 12. " Shakspeare Platonizes," by W. Watkiss Lloyd.
(Philosophizing upon the passage in the *Merchant of
Venice*, " But whilst this muddy *vesture of decay*, &c."
and treating of the Pythagorean conception of the
harmony of the spheres, and Plato's poetizing it),.

,, Ibid. "Runaway's Eyes," by Dr. C. M. Ingleby.
(Reply to Dr. Nicholson's letter on March 31st, and maintains adoption of *runaways* of the Second Quarto.)

1877. May 26. "Runaway's Eyes," by Lewis Campbell.
(That it means *runaways*, a sort of persons most likely to be abroad at night).

,, July 7. "Shakespeare and Caxton," by E. Scott.
(Giving parallel passages from Caxton's "Game of Chess" and Shakespeare's Plays).

,, Aug. 4. "Shakspeare Notes," by W. Watkiss Lloyd.
(On the etymology of a few words.)

,, Aug. 18. *"Shakspeare and Milton," by Prof: J. W. Hales.
(Showing by extracts from Milton's Poems, the influence of Shakespeare).

,, Sept. 8. *"Shakespeare and Mucedorus," by J. Payne Collier.
(Maintains that Shakespeare wrote a part of this play).

,, *Ibid* "Shakspeare Notes," by W. Watkiss Lloyd.
(On words "*though*" or "*through*" and "*congreeing*" in Henry V. Act I, s. 2. Advocates *though* and *agree*).

,, *Ibid* "Father Parsons, &c." by Dr. A. Jessopp.
(Not exactly within the scope of this list, but useful in connection with letter, under date in *The Academy*, March 8, 1879.)

,, Nov. 3. *"Stratford-on-Avon in 1605," by Professor J. W. Hales.
(On the possible influence of the *Gunpowder Plot* upon Shakespeare and his writings).

,, Nov. 10. "Shakespeare and the Dutch Dramatists," by E. W. Gosse.
(On early Dutch Dramatists imitating Shakespeare.)

,, Dec. 15. *"The Merchant of Venice, in 1652," by Professor J. W. Hales.

1878. Feb. 16. "Shakspeare Notes," by W. Watkiss Lloyd.
(On the line "Most busie lest, when I doe it," in "The Tempest." Suggests or rather *supports, least* with a *comma* after *busy*.)

,, April 6. *"The Merry Wives of Windsor," by P. A. Daniel.
(On the entanglement of the Plot.)

,, July 6. *"Coriolanus," by P. A. Daniel.
(On complication of the Plot.)

,, July 20. Review of "Reprints of Single Plays of Shakspeare," viz.:—*A Midsummer Night's Dream*, and *Julius Cæsar*, edited by W. Aldis Wright, M.A.; *A Midsummer Night's Dream* and *Hamlet*, edited by S. Neil; *Coriolanus*, edited by J. Colville, M.A.; and *King John*, edited by F. G. Fleay, M.A.
(Highly and justly commendatory.)

,, Aug. 24. *"Shakespeare Notes," by W. Watkiss Lloyd.
(Textual emendations: King John, Timon of Athens, &c.)

,, Sept. 7. "A Noting of Shakespeare Notes," by Dr. B. Nicholson.
(Differs from views of Mr. W. W. Lloyd, in re "*new untrimmed* bride" in King John, Act III, s. 1, l. 209. Mr. Lloyd says, "*trimmed up*" is a current phrase for the height of feminine adornment." Dr. Nicholson suggests, "a new, or untouched and untrimmed bride.")

1878. Sept. 14. *"Hamlet," by Professor J. W. Hales.
(Quotes a passage from *Father Hubbard's Tales*, 1604, as the *earliest* allusion to this play if *a nest of boys*, is a form of Shakespeare's "aery of children, little eyasses.")

„   *Ibid*   "Notings Renoted," by W. Watkiss Lloyd.
(A rejoinder to Dr. Nicholson's letter of the 24th August. Athenæum.)

„   Sept. 21. *"Early Reference to a Passage in ' Pericles,'" by A. H. Bullen.
(Cites John Day's *Law's Tricks*, a play, 1608. States *Pericles* published 1609, but acted as early as 1607).

„   Sept. 28. *"Father Hubbard and Hamlet," by F. J. Furnivall
(Differs from Professor Hales *sub.*, Sept. 14—that *nest* cannot stand as a Hamlet allusion.)

„   Nov. 23. *"John Florio." (The translator of Montaigne). by C. Elliot Browne.
(An account of Florio, to whom Shakespeare is *supposed* to have been indebted for his *Holofernes*).

„   *Ibid* *"The Taming of the Shrew," by F. G. Fleay.
(On the date of this play).

1879. Jan. 4. *"The Moor of Denmark," by G. Bullen.
(Was Claudius, King of Denmark, the uncle of Hamlet, of a dark complexion ?—Believes he was *decidedly so*.)

„   Jan. 11. *"Hamlet," *a*. 1., *s*. 4., *l*. 5., by K. Elze.
(The word "indeed" should be spoken by Hamlet.)

„   *Ibid.* *"The Moor of Denmark," by Dr. B. Nicholson.
(Differs *in toto* from Mr. Bullen. Jan. 4th.)

„   Feb. 15. *"Another Tragedy by Shakspeare," by J. Payne Collier.
(That "A Warning for Fair Women" was by Shakespeare, but had a coadjutor or coadjutors.)

„   Feb. 22. *"A Warning for Faire Women," by J. W. M Gibbs.
(Points out Mr. R. Simpson's anticipations of Mr. Payne Collier's "find," and that he, in 1878, suggested Shakespeare's probable connection with it.)

„   *Ibid.* *Ditto, by F. S. Ellis.
(States "that Mr. C.'s copy is not unique, Mr. H. Huth having one in his library.")

„   March 1. *Ditto, by J. Payne Collier.
(" My belief that Shakespeare was concerned in the original production . . . . . was published 48 years ago." In reply to Mr. Gibbs.)

„   *Ibid.* *"The Moor of Denmark," by G. Bullen.
(A reply to Dr. Nicholson, of Jan. 11.)

„   *Ibid.* Ditto, by Dr. B. Nicholson.
(Original position maintained against an attack by Mr. Ebsworth.)

„   July 19. "Shakespeare Notes." "Coriolanus," by W. Watkiss Lloyd.
(Several textual emendations and guesses.)

„   Dec. 13. *"On Fauors==Ill-favoured," in Julius Cæsar, by Dr. K. Elze.

879. Dec. 27. *"On Fauors=Mavors or Mars=God of Battle,"
     by Robert Browning.
      (*Vide, Notes and Queries, sub.* 1880 April 24).

1880. Jan. 10. *"On *Fauors* in Julius Cæsar, 1., iii., 128—130."
     by F. C. Birkbeck Terry. (Suggests, for *Is.
     Fauors,* read *In's Fauors !!*)

,, Feb. 21. *"On Swinburne and Hamlet and Macbeth," by
     J. Spedding.
      (In opposition to the statement of the reviewer of Swin-
      burne's "Study of Shakespeare," that "no one seems
      to have compared Hamlet with Macbeth," the writer
      contends that Hartley Coleridge has anticipated some
      of Mr. Swinburne's best points, in his "Essay on the
      Character of Hamlet," and quotes from "Essays and
      Marginalia." The editorial note maintains original
      position, and differs from Hartley Coleridge's criticism
      which is "allied to the German misconception about
      the nature of Shakspeare's marvellous imagination.")

,, April 10. *"The Life of Shakespeare," by J. O. Halliwell-
     Phillipps.
      (Announcing the publication of a series of folio volumes,
      entitled "Contributions towards a Life of Shakes-
      peare," provided there is sufficient interest taken in
      the subject to encourage him.)

"The Academy."

1870. April 9. "Shakespeare and the Emblem Writers," by
     F. Palliser.
      (A review of a book of this title, by Mr. Henry Green,
      M.A. The reviewer says, "The works of the emblem
      writers were early translated into English, and the
      object of Mr. Green's work is to show that Shakespeare
      was among the host of emblem students, and that he
      borrowed their help and imagery, either directly or
      indirectly;" and in defining "*emblem,*" he says, "the
      emblem or 'impressa' was a special personal attribute
      which the knight wore in the field and in the tourna-
      ment, embroidered on his surcoat and the trappings
      of his horse, and had inscribed on his plate, his jewels,
      and his household furniture."

1871. June 1. *"The Sources of Shakespeare, in Novels, Tales,
     and Legends," by Felix Liebrecht.
      (An interesting and valuable review of Simrock's work
      on this subject.)

1874. Mar. 28. "Mr. Fleay on Metrical Tests," by Mr. F. G. Fleay.
      (Merely a correction of a table inserted in *The Academy* for
      March 21. "calculated from the metrical table in my
      [Mr. Fleay's] first paper for the Shakspere Society
      [*New*]." Gives also *Proportion of Rhyme in Verse Scenes
      in Blank Verse,* by this writer's *rhyme test.*)

,, Aug. 29. "A passage in Lear," by F. J. Furnivall.
      (A note on the meaning of "challenge." Says, upon the
      line "where Nature doth with merit CHALLENGE," the
      last word means "where your natural relation to, and
      love for me, claim my bounty by deserving it.")

,, Sept. 19. *"Posthumous" in "Cymbeline," by F. J. Furnivall.
      (Discussion on accentuation of *posthumous.* Attack on
      Mr. Fleay's *Rhyme* test. Mr. Fleay accentuates the
      "u," and Furnivall the "o," in this word. The writer
      however attempts at *hard hitting,* and the Editor says,
      "We cannot receive any further letters on this subject.")

,, Nov. 14. *"Shakspere not the Part-author of Ben Jonson's
     'Sejanus,'" by Dr. Brinsley Nicholson.
      (Denying the statement of Capell, W. Whalley and others,
      that Shakespeare *was* a Part-author.)

1874. Dec. 12. *"An Allusion in Hamlet. Act. iii., s. 2." by F. J. Furnivall.
(On origin and meanings of "The Croaking Rauen,"="*Is the Ghost of Hamlet's Father.*")

,, Dec. 19. *Ditto, by R. Simpson.
(A comment on the remarks of the above, and says "the work of commenting should be postponed the work of gathering materials." Objects to the comment of Mr. Furnivall.)

1875. Jan. 2. *"A Passage in Hamlet," by R. Simpson.
(On origin of the line "the croaking raven doth bellow for revenge," differs from Mr. Furnivall, who said it is taken from the unknown old *Hamlet*, and Mr. Simpson says, " I have proved it to be a parody of lines in the old *Richard III.*")

,, Feb. 20. *"The Original of Shakespeare's 'Othello,'" by E. H. Pickersgill.
(Maintains that the play coincides with Cinthio's Novel of the Moor of Venice.)

,, Sept. 18. "Shakspeare and Queen Elizabeth's Favourites," by F. J. Furnivall.
(A purely conjectural communication. Attempts to show, by quoting passages from *Much Ado about Nothing*, *Act* III., *sc.* 1, *l.* 9—11, and Henry V., *Act* V., *l.* 24—25, and 30—32, that the allusions are, in the former, to "some insolent favourite of the time, A.D. 1600;" and in the latter, to " Essex's assured success, to be in Ireland.")

,, Oct. 9. *"Essays on Shakespeare." (A long and critical review of Dr. Karl Elze's work) by Prof. J. W. Hales.
(Especially opposes Dr. K. E.'s theory of Shakespeare's continental travels.)

,, Dec. 18. *"Hamlet's Age," by W. Minto.
(Tries to prove he was *seventeen*; "I am prepared to admit eighteen; I might even, though with reluctance, give in to nineteen; but there I draw the line, and I am quite willing to maintain my original position of seventeen.")

,, Dec. 25. *"Hamlet's Age," by Prof. E. Dowden and F. J. Furnivall.
(Mr. Minto's view of "17 years" discussed. Prof. Dowden inclines to "25 years of age." Mr. Furnivall inclines to "quite a young man, and in the gravedigger's scene, 30 years of age.)

1876. Jan. 8. "Mr. Swinburne and Mr. Spedding—Shakspere's 'Henry VIII.'" by F. J. Furnivall.
(An attempt at a satirical attack upon Mr. Swinburne's position, that this play is *entirely* Shakespeare's and not *part Fletcher*.)

,, Jan. 15. "'King Henry VIII.' and the Ordeal by Metre," by A. C. Swinburne.
(A most trenchant reply to preceding.)

,, Jan. 29. Ditto, by F. J. Furnivall.
(Controversy continued, but the true interests of Shakespearean study not advanced. From a literary point of view the satire is weak and strained.)

---

[3] Subsequently enlarged and published as a book, entitled "Elizabethan Demonology."

1879. March 8. *" Father Parsons, Falstaff, and Shakspere," by C. Elliot Browne. [4]
(On some obscure points about the pedigree of Falstaff.)

,, Mar. 15. " Shakspere's ' Hot at Hand.' " Julius Cæsar, Act IV., s. ii, l. 23-4. By E. H. Hickey.
(That "hot at hand" signifies "chafing against (the restraining) Hand.")

,, April 5. *" Hamlet's Leaping into Ophelia's Grave," by A. H. Huth.
(Does not agree with Mr. Moy Thomas with regard to an incidental remark that the "elegy on Burbage cannot be authentic.")

,, July 5. " Shakspere and the Bible," by J. B. Selkirk.
(Charges the Rev. C. Bullock with plagiarizing from his book Bible Truths and Shakespearean Parallels.)

,, July 12. Do., by Rev. C. Bullock.
(Reply to preceding; an explanation. A trivial quarrel.)

,, Aug. 23. *" On Oldcastle and Falstaff," by C. Elliott Browne.
(A continuation of this writer's letter of the 8th March, and asks: What were Oldcastle's personal relations to Henry V., 2 ?)

,, Oct. 25. A short Notice of Mr. J. G. Herr's Notes on the Text of Shakspere. (In Notes and News column.)
(Points out a few absurd emendations.)

1880. Jan. 3. *" Review of Swinburne's "Study of Shakespeare," by Prof. E. Dowden.

,, ,, 10. *Reply to same by A. C. Swinburne.

,, ,, ,, Attack on Mr. Swinburne and his book, by F. J. Furnivall.

,, ,, 17. Reply to Mr. Swinburne's letter, by Professor E. Dowden.

,, Mar. 27. " A Passage in ' 2 Henry IV.' " by W. J. Rolfe.
(Opposes the Cambridge editors in ending the fourth scene of act iv., with line 132, and says, " In my new edition now printing, I make the change of scene and insert the Exeunt.)

,, April 10. " A Passage in 2, Henry IV," by W. Aldis Wright.
(Gives reasons for the Cambridge Editors making Scene V begin with the line, "Let there be no noise made, my gentle friends.")

,, April 24. Review of Mr. T. A. Spalding's "Elizabethan Demonology," by F. J. Furnivall.
(In the course of the review, Mr. Furnivall agrees with Mr. Spalding in interpreting "Assume a virtue, if you have it not," as meaning Acquire, &c. The book is highly commended.)

,, May 1. On a passage in Hamlet III, iv., 160, (assume a virtue if you have it not.) by W. Aldis Wright.
(Objects to reading assume, to acquire. Maintains it means "to put on something external to oneself, a form or shape.")

---

[4] Vide " The Athenæum," sub. 1877, September 8th.

1880. May 8.   Ditto   ditto   by T. A. Spalding.
(Says *assume*, means to *acquire*.)

,,   ,,   ,,   Ditto   ditto   by F. J. Furnivall.
(Agrees with Mr. Spalding.)

,,   ,,   15.   Ditto   ditto   by W. Aldis Wright.
(Maintains original position).

,,   ,,   Ditto   ditto   by Professor J. W. Hales.
(Supports Mr. A. W. Wright's view.)

,,   ,,   Ditto   ditto   by L. M. Griffiths.
(Opposes Mr. Spalding's view.)

"The Theatre."

1879. Feb.   *"The Emphasis Capitals of Shakspere."
(A review of an edition of Hamlet, with remarks on this subject, by A. Park Paton. Commendatory.)

,,   March.   *"Another Tragedy by Shakspere."
(A traverse of Mr. J. Payne Collier's statement that the alleged spurious Shakespeare's play of "*A Warning for Faire Women*" is *genuine*; in this *hypothesis*, Mr. Collier was unsupported by anyone.)

,,   April.   *"The Portraits in *Hamlet*."
(Mr. H. Irving's article in the *Nineteenth Century* discussed. Arguments advanced against his views of *mental* pictures. *Vide, The Nineteenth Century.* Feb., 1879.)

,,   Nov.   *"On Shylock and other Stage Jews," by F. Hawkins.

,,   Dec.   *"The Character of Shylock," a series of views by Theodore Martin; an Actor; F. J. Furnivall; F. Marshall; James Spedding; Israel Davies; D. Anderson; and F. Hawkins.

1880. January. *"Shylock in Germany," Part I., by W. Beatty-Kingston.

,,   February. Ditto, Part II. (concluded.)
(An account of German interpretation and acting of this character.)

,,   June.   "Shakespeare at Home," by David Anderson.
(A slight account of the Festival held at Stratford-on-Avon, on the 23rd April last, and commendatory of Mr. Barry Sullivan's generosity in giving his services and those of his company as a free gift toward the Fund for the completion of the Memorial Theatre.)

"The Antiquary." (*Old Issue.*)

1873. Jan. 11.   "Shakespeare Commentators," by J. Perry.
(A short biographical notice of "Zachariah Jackson, and account of his *Shakespeare's Genius Justified*, [1819]; and, *A Few Concise Examples of Errors Corrected in Shakespeare's Plays*.)

,,   June 21.   "Shakespeare's Character of Polonius," by William Myers.
(Says, to represent Polonius on the stage as a kind of feeble-minded, lean, and slippered pantaloon, whose chief business is to raise a laugh," is inconsistent "with the wisdom and manliness of the advice Polonius gives his son, and the speeches he makes at other points of the play.")

1873. Sept. 20. "Shakespeare as a Theatre Proprietor," by H. Wright.

(Says "The opportune discovery of J. O. Halliwell, recently made and announced in the *Antiquary*, see page 111, *ante*, that Shakespeare was *neither a Proprietor nor a Sharer in the Globe or the Blackfriars Theatres* is one of considerable importance." The writer therefrom infers that Shakespeare must have been an actor of a superior order, to enable us to account for the wealth he amassed.)

,, Nov. 8. "Shakespeare's Portrait," by H. Wright.

(A description of the known portraits of the dramatist, with the writer's view upon their genuineness.)

"The Antiquary." *(New Issue.)*

1880. January. *"Early Mention of Hamlet," by J. Payne Collier.

(Mentions a MS. list of Books, and one called, *Hamlet's Historie*, dated 1595. Belonging to the Trevelyan family.)

,, Feb. "The Early and Unknown Mention of Hamlet," by F. J. Furnivall.

(Says that Mr. Collier will find this mentioned in the new edition of Dr. Ingleby's *Centurie of Prayse*, p. 453.)

,, March "Was the Cheetah known to Shakespeare?" by Walter Tomlinson.

(On "*Cheater* call you him?" in Henry VI, Part 2, Act ii, s. 4. Dr. Johnson says of this word, "one who cheats," and an "Escheator" [Dictionary]. Suggests Shakespeare meant the Cheetah, "that spotted, cat-like animal, so well known in India.")

,, Ibid. *"Romeo and Juliet," by W. Ransome.

(Disputes Mr. Furnivall's statement in the "Leopold Shakspere," that its source is Arthur Brooke's versification of Boaistuan's 3rd tale in his *Histories Tragiques*, 1562; and says that Boaistuan's work was not published till five years after Brooke's poem).

,, May "Was the Cheetah known to Shakespeare?" by Dr. B. Nicholson.

(Ridicules Mr. Tomlinson's suggestion, and holds the obvious meaning—a cheat.)

"Notes and Queries."[5]

1871. July 15. "Shakespeariana, Three Explanations and Two Probable Opinions," by Dr. B. Nicholson.

("Drums *demurely* wake." *Antony and Cleopatra*, Act IV, sc. 9. Differs from the *Cambridge* Shakespeare Editors, and restores to the original, the word from their alteration of, *mutiny*. "I'll keep my *Stables, &c.*," *Winter's Tale*, Act II, s. i. Says it means that, Antigonus "will be coupled with her [his wife] as hounds are, and so keep her from straying." This communication is continued, and concludes in the number for July 29th.)

,, Aug. 5. "Shakespeare's Rosencrantz," by Walter Thornbury.

(Calls attention to the fact that a "Danish nobleman, named Rosenkrantz, attended the Danish Ambassador into England on the accession of King James I," and says "It is almost certain that *Hamlet* (first published in its complete form in 1604) was written either immediately before or at the succession of James I. (1603).

[5] It would make a book of itself, were all the items of Shakespeareana given, only a very few are selected; the reader will do well to turn to the Indexes to this valuable journal.

1871. Aug. 17. " Peacock ; Paddock ; Puttock ; Pajocke ; Polack,"
by Dr. R. G. Latham.
(Suggests *Polack* in lieu of *Paiock*. [*Hamlet*, Act III, s. ii,
l. 295). Says the word suggested, is *Danish* in form.
Its primary sense is a *Pole*, a native of Poland, and its
secondary meaning is *blackguard*, a Philistine. Those
interested, should turn to Bulloch's *Studies on the Text
of Shakespeare*, 1878 pp. 228-9 for other very *curious*
readings of this passage.)

"   *Ibid.*   " Shakspere Notes."—Knight's Pictorial Shakspere—*Cymbeline*. *Act* I, sc. ii, by J.A.G.
(Says " Mr. Knight says the sense [of this passage] is
obscure." This writer alters punctuation to remove
obscurity.)

"   Aug. 26.   " The Latest Shakspearean Discovery," by
Walter Thornbury.
(Comments upon a statement in *The Athenæum* of July 8th,
1871, " that Mr. Halliwell has lately discovered that
Shakspeare and 'fellows' were ordered by James I.,
to attend the Spanish Ambassador at Somerset House
for upwards of a fortnight, in August, 1604 ; and
Mr. Halliwell expresses a hope that some of the readers
of *The Athenæum* might be acquainted with a detailed
account of the visit of the Ambassador, in which
further information on the subject might be recorded.
Mr. Thornbury then gives a rather full account of the
banquet and entertainment given by James I. to the
Constable of Castile—Juan Fernandez de Velasco,
Duke de Frias,—extracted from' Mr. W. B. Rye's
England as Seen by Foreigners, 1865 : in which, however,
the mention of Shakespeare or his fellows *does not
occur*.)

"   Sept. 2.   Ditto, by J. O. Halliwell.
(Says, " the genuineness of the manuscript which has
yielded the 'latest discovery,' is beyond suspicion, and
the complete texts of this and of several other papers
of equal curiosity, but of greater value, will be included
in a forthcoming new work on the Life of Shakespeare.")

"   Sept. 23.   "Peacock ; Paddock ; Puttock ; Pajock ; Polack ;"
by T. McGarth.
(Differs from Dr. Latham's emendation of *paiock* in *Hamlet*,
and says, " the word *pajock* is misunderstood, simply
because it is mis-pronounced *pa-jock*, but substitute
what is clearly the correct syllabication, *paj-ock*, and
all is made clear. *Paj=patch*, a contemptuous term for
a person—a mean fellow ; and *ock*, diminutive ; *pajock*,
or *patchock*, a paltry clown.")

"   Oct. 21.   Ditto, by Dr. B. Nicholson.
(Advances reasons for adopting the *peajock=peacock*
reading, and *guesses* about Shakespeare's preference
for using this word instead of " ass.")

1872. July 13.   " Titus Andronicus : Ira Aldridge," by N.
(Relates the writer's witnessing of Aldridge's [the African
Roscius] performance of Aaron in this play. " The
playbill had a long paragraph, which defended the
authorship of Shakspeare and threw the gauntlet at
all doubters.")

"   Sept. 7.   " Shakespeare : Macbeth, iii., iv., 104," by John
Addis.
(Upon the words " Absorbed it." Prefers the old reading,
" If trembling, I inhabit then.")

"   *Ibid.*   Ditto, by C. A. W.
(Adopts Pope's reading of *inhibit*, and changes *then* to *thee*.)

1872.	Oct. 12.	"Shakspeariana: the Outward and Inward Eye." (*King John*, Act II., sc. 2), for *outward eye*, by W. L. Rushton. (Shows difference between *outward eye* and *eye of reason* or *inward* eye.)
„	*Ibid.*	"Heart cannot Conceive," by W. L. Rushton. (Thinks Shakspeare may in this passage [*Macbeth*, Act ii., sc. 2,] refer to a passage, cited, from Lyly's *Euphues*; but the writer has very carelessly, if he knew it, omitted the *exact reference*.)
„	*Ibid.*	"Imperious," *Hamlet*, Act v., sc. 1., by F. Rule. (Points out the reading of the *Folios* of *Imperial* Cæsar, Letter of no importance.)
„	*Ibid.*	"Hawk and Handsaw," by R. W. Hackwood. (An attempt at sarcastic wit, at the expense of the tedious emendators of this and the *Eysl* difficulty in *Hamlet*.)
„	Nov. 30.	*"Shakespeariana."—"Hank," "Handsaw," &c., by J. A. Picton. (Maintains *handsaw* as the right word).
.,	Dec. 14.	"Shakspeariana," by W. L. Rushton. (Illustrates a few passages in *Twelfth Night*; *Love's Labour's Lost*; *First Part of King Henry IV.*; and *Romeo and Juliet*, by extracts from the *Toxophilus* of Ascham, the *Euphues* of Lyly, *The Arte of Poesie* by Puttenham, and *Coke's Reports*. This communication is of *no* value, as the writer has again omitted to give *exact* references to page, etc.)
1873.	April 19.	"Shakspeariana: Conjectural Notes on Shakspeare and other Writers," by John Addis. (Does not agree with all the derivations of F. J. V., in 4th S., xi., 210; takes the following words and suggests meanings:— BISSON—*blind*; "*Aroint*,"—says "Douce seems to me in the right direction when he connects aroint with A. S. *ryne*;" *Embossed*=embushed, the word however has *puzzled* this learned emendator, which is perhaps not singular. *Cock-a-hoop*="to take out the spigot and lay it upon the top of the barrel," he consequently does not agree in its present slang interpretation of "in high spirits.")
	Ibid.	"Aroint; Embost; Talents; and Cock-a-hoop," by F. J. V. (If his conjectures be right, *aroins* and *aroint* will correspond to the two French forms, *erené* and *éreinté*. *Embost*,—of this word, F. J. V, says, "so far as I am aware, it is only found as a past participle; therefore, if a man said 'the stag is *en abois*,' that might easily be corrupted into 'the stag is *en* or *en bois*,' and when the derivation was forgotten, a participle termination might be given to it, and it would become 'the stag is *embost*.'" *Talents*—of no concern, as it does not belong in this letter to *Shakspeariana*. *Cock-a-hoop*="Cock of the Dung-heap!!" Such emendations and derivations are evidently *indispensable* to some Shakespearean students, but it will after all be well to avoid them.)
„	May 10.	"The Earliest Mention of Shakspeare," by C. Elliot Browne. (Upon the "Polimanteia" of W(illiam) C(larke), wherein is the earliest mention of the poet, and the writer remarks that the allusion is mentioned in the *margin*.)

1873. June 7. "Shakspeariana: Shakspeare and Burns," by F. Rule.
(Merely points out a few parallels showing resemblance beween these two poets.)

" Ibid. "As You Like It," by F. Rule.
(Upon the word, *having*, being a *substantive*, in *Twelfth Night, Act* iii., *sc.* 4, 379, and *As You Like It, Act* ii., *sc.* 3, 61.)

" Ibid. Ditto, by John Addis.
(The passage in *As You Like It, Act* iii., *sc.* 2, 193, cited to illustrate the controversy continued from 4th S., xi., 424, upon the meaning of "having a beard," and maintains that *having* means *possession*.)

" Ibid. Ditto, by W. J. C.
(Quotes from *Macbeth, Act* i., *sc.* 3, to show that "having" is frequently used as a substantive in Elizabethan English.)

" Ibid. Ditto, by Erem.
(Says ' Having," according to Johnson, is *noun substantive* and has three distinct senses.)

" Ibid. Ditto, by CCC. X. I.
(Shows, by quoting from C. Knight's edition, that the suggestion given by S. in the former number, is not original, but has been disposed of by that Shakespearean scholar.)

" Ibid. "Cock-a-Hoop," by C. A. W.
(Ridicules the guesses, etc., of the previous correspondents [in April 19th] and restores the passage to its legitimate meaning, ' cock-a-hoop is cock-a-top, cock-a-crest,' = elated beyond reason.)

" July 12. "The Prosody of Shakspeare in its National Aspect," by Hyde Clarke.
(A very interesting article upon the use of alliteration. He says, "There is one point I would wish to call attention to, in the prosody of Shakespeare, that is, a continuation of Anglo-Saxon traditions and forms. Its great principle is alliteration; and although some of the canons of the Skalds are not adopted, yet, in the main, the structure is Anglo-Saxon in Shakspeare, as it is in the continuous series of English poetry to our own day." He then illustrates his thesis. *Vide* also a letter upon the *Staff Rime*, &c., in *The Academy* of March 1st, 1879, by Dr. Karl Blind.)

" Ibid. "Embossed," by F. J. V.
(A continuation of guesswork upon the meaning of this word, following a communication by F. J. Furnivall in a previous number, and says, "the old derivation from *bosse*=a hump; a bubble, adopted by Mr. Furnivall, is the more probable one, and concludes a long letter thus:—" In conclusion, my contention now is that *emboss*, in all the passages in which it is found, is derived from *bosse*, and in no sense from *bois* or *boite*.")

" Ibid. Ditto, by Ralph N. James,
(Upon the forms of this word, and says that "*embossed*, derived from *bosse*, differs little from our modern *embossed*.")

1874. Feb. 7. "On Shakespeare's Pastoral Name," by Dr. B. Nicholson.
(Favours some of Mr. Elliot Browne's arguments in *Notes and Queries*, 4th S. xii, 509; upon *Philisides*, being Sir Philip Sidney; *good Melibee*, being first applied to Walsingham, and after his death, Chettle called Marston "young Melibee," but Drayton's application of this epithet 'to some one who was either related to, or a great friend of, Sidney," shows that Chettle was not followed on an authority. *Melicert* is suggested to have been first applied, to a statesman or person of eminence, probably Burleigh, and after his death, Chettle applied it to "Shakspeare of the honied muse.")

1879. May 10. "Marston and Shakspeare," by Dr. B. Nicholson.
(Takes words from *Hamlet*. iv., 2, ll. 14-20, and *All's Well*, iv., 2, l. 73 [*spundge* and *braide* respectively], to show that Marston in his *Scourge of Villanie* [1598], preceded Shakspeare in their use.)

, *Ibid.* "The Tempest," *Act* i., sc. 2, ll. 168-9, by Dr. B. Nicholson.
(Quotes "from the first part of Homily xxxiii, to show that 'foote,'" of this passage is used in the same sense "as though the *foot* must judge of the head.")

May 17. "Shakespeariana: A few Notes on Othello," by R. M. Spence, M.A.
(Emendates *wife* [*Act* i., sc. 1, l. 21], to *wise*; *motion* [*Act* i., sc. 2. l. 75], to *emotion*; *intentirely* [*Act* i., sc. 3. l. 155], to *distinctirely*; and prefers *First Folio* reading of *Act* iv., sc. 2, l. 54, with a transposition of "for" and "of," to that of the *Globe* Edition.)

Ibid. "Macbeth . . . with Notes and Emendations by Harry Rowe . . . Master of a Puppet Show," by J. M. Hubbard.
(Supports the hypothesis that this book was written by Dr. Hunter of York. *Vide* List of Books, *sub.* 1797, *infra*.)

July 5. "Shakespeariana: 'Ancient' and 'Scamels,'" by J. D.
(Upon the meaning of the word "ancient" in 1 *Henry IV.*, iv., 2, and *Othello*, i., sc. 1, and says it means "a personal attendant or body squire;" and *Scamels*, in the *Tempest*, ii., 2, he interprets as *filberts*, and bristles his letter with formidable Scandinavian roots.)

July 12. "Shakespeariana: 'To Make a Man,'" by J. D.
(Takes *make a man*, from *The Tempest*, ii., 2; *All's Well*, iv., 3; *Twelfth Night*, iii, 4; and *Winter's Tale*, iii., 3, and thinks it means "to endow a man with wealth or honour.")

Ibid. "The Crux of Sonnet cxvi.," by Bibliothecary.
(Submits that *height* means "to promise or vow.")

Aug. 9. "Shakspeare in Gloucestershire," by Adin Williams.
(Supports the idea that the poet visited his relations at Dursley, in that shire. Of course purely guesswork.)

,, Aug. 23. Ditto, by O. W. Tancock.
(Attacks some of the statements of preceding writer, and shows briefly that Marlowe's writings are "particularly free from provincialisms," and further that his assertion that *Edward II.* is "a peculiarly Gloucestershire subject," is unsupported, as is also "that Shakspeare advised Marlowe to write his *Edward II.*)

Ibid. Ditto, by P. J. E. Gantillon.
(Upsets A. Williams's idea that *Perke's*, of 2 *Henry IV.*, Act v., sc. 1, is meant for a house on Stinchcombe Hill, [Glou:] by saying that "Perks is a very common name in this place [Cheltenham], also that there is another Wodmancote in this county.")

, *Ibid.* Ditto, by J. W. B. P.
(Says, "so late as 1812 the Hill Stinchcombe was in the occupation of the Purcha [or Perkis] family.)

Aug. 30. "Disappointed Hamlet." *Act* 1, sc. 5, *l.* 77, by F. J. F.
(Adduces an argument to prove that this word means *unshriven*.)

1880. Jan. 17. "Undiscovered Country," in Hamlet, by E. Marshall.
(Conjectural, of course).

,   Jan. 31. "Shakespeariana.."—Readings of text in "Cymbeline," by R. M. Spence, M.A.

,,   Feb.   7. *"The Familiars of the Macbeth Witches," by Dr. R. Nicholson.
(Conjectural.)

,.   Feb. 21. "Shakespeariana: Macbeth, V., iii., 55," by Dr. B. Nicholson.
(On the word cyme in this passage. Suggests "Cynca or Cynce, the Canina Brassica, the mercury, French and dog mercuries, etc., of our older authors." The leaves of mercury.)

,,   Feb. 28. "Historical Names in Shakspeare's Plays," by S. L. Lee.
(Takes Birom and Longarille, in Love's Labour's Lost, and says they "are taken directly from contemporary French history." Antonio and Sebastian were probably suggested by Don Antonio, "a fugitive pretender to the crown of Portugal," especially as regards the one in the Merchant of Venice, "and may have been the original of Two Gentlemen of Verona; Much Ado about Nothing; The Tempest; and Twelfth Night. Sebastian named after the Sebastian the "last King of Portugal.")

,,   Mar. 13. "Shakspeariana: Macbeth, v., iii., 55," by W. Whiston.
(Submits with "much diffidence" that the Cyme of Dr. Nicholson may be a corruption of Cynanchum, from which the French scammony is prepared. This may be called Cymerical criticism, which may well be purged.)

,,   Ibid.   *"The Legend of Zarqa." (Origin of the legend of Birnam Wood), by W. F. Prideaux.
(Very interesting.)

,.   Mar. 27. "Shakespeare's 'Midsummer Night's Dream,' and Goethe's 'Walpurgisnachtstraum,'" by H. Krebs.
(States that Puck has evidently been suggested to Goethe by Shakspere. Controverts Simrock, "if he denies that Shakspere derived it [the name of Titania] from classical mythology," and mentions Ovid [in Metamorphoses iii., 173] calling Diana, Titania.)

,,   Ibid.   "Shakespeariana: The Crux of Sonnet cxvi." (vide July 12, 1879), by Dr. B. Nicholson.
(Objects to Bibliothecary's correction, and takes the word hight to be higth_ height, and says, "one's whereabouts at sea, or at least, one's lattitude is ascertained by taking the meridian height of a celestial body.")

,,   Ibid.   Ditto, by B. C.
(Coincides with the preceding.)

,,   Ibid.   "To Sag." Macbeth, v., iii., 10, by T. Bayne.
(Points out a use of the participle sagged or seggit, in Scotland, as when "a haystack that has been borne down and thrawn by the winter's storms," it is said, "it is seggit.")

,,   April 24. "Shakspeariana: All's Well, iv., ii., 73," by Dr. B. Nicholson.
(On the word braide. Merely citing the use of this word by other writers; does not alter the sense of deceitful.)

1880.	*Ibid.*	"**All's Well that Ends Well, iv., ii.,**" by R. R.

(Very triumphant. This writer has at last hit upon the right meaning of "rope;" quotes from *Naps upon Parnassus*, 1658, A., vi.—

"———— I ne're shall grope
It out. but by *Ariadne's rope*."

He says, "there you are at once. the passage explains itself." and yet he goes on further to explain!)

,,	*Ibid.*	"'**Via**' in the Merchant of Venice, II., ii., 9," by Dr. B. Nicholson.

(Says it is an Italian word [vea, a nautical term] and "was apparently spoken unanimously, and like the paviours' 'Hoh !'")

,,	*Ibid.*	"**Sag**," by Celer.

(Mentions its being recorded by Halliwell, and means to *sink down.*)

,,	*Ibid.*	Ditto, by D. G. Sexton.

(Mentions its use in Norfolk: "anything hanging loosely down.")

,,	*Ibid.*	*"**Julius Cæsar, I., iii., 128-9,** by Hyde Clarke.

(Suggests *It*, for *Is* Fauors.)

,,	May 15.	*"**The Alleged Pre-Shakspearian 'Hamlet,'**" by Dr. C. M. Ingleby.

(Follows *Notes and Queries*. 5th S.. iv., 421. In opposition to Mr. Elliot Browne. "I propose to say a few words in support of my own firm belief that there was a drama on the subject of 'Hamlet' long before Shakspeare wrote his first sketch. I do not commit myself to any opinion on the question whether Shakspeare took the older play as the *prima stamina* of his own, nor yet whether the quarto of 1603 does substantially, though with much dislocation and interpolation. represent his first sketch." and concludes, after giving many quotations in support of his position, by submitting "that this belief in a pre-Shakspearian *Hamlet* is a natural and rational conclusion.")

"The Nineteenth Century."

1877.	April.	*"**The Third Murderer in Macbeth.**" (An Actor's Notes on Shakespeare. No. 1.), by Henry Irving.

(Mr. Irving attempts to arrive at the identity of the *third murderer*. but utterly fails through mistaking interpolated stage directions in the play, for Shakespeare's.)

,,	May.	* "**Hamlet and Ophelia.**" (An Actor's Notes on Shakespeare. No. 2), by Henry Irving.

(Attempts to solve the questions in relation to *Act* iii., *sc.* 1:—

I.—Whether Hamlet knew throughout the scene that he was watched by the King and Polonius ?

2.—Whether Ophelia knew that her father and the King were eaves-droppers ?

In reference to question 1. the writer blunders in a curious manner. He says:—"the text tells us that he knew he was being watched from the first, for in the quartos of 1603 and 1604 [the complete play]. Hamlet enters before the *exeunt* words of Polonius to the King—'Let's withdraw, my lord.' The fact is, the quarto of 1603 *does not* contain either the *exeunt* or the words, "Let's withdraw, my lord." In the 1604 quarto, "enter Hamlet" occurs *one* line before the retirement of Polonius and the King. Upon the second question, Mr. Irving argues that Ophelia *did not* know the King and her father were watching. For a critical yet fair examination of this article by Mr. Moy Thomas, see *The Athenæum*, May 5th, 1877.)

1878. January. *" Shakespeare in France," by Dr. John Doran F.S.A.
(A valuable historical account of the representation of Shakespeare's plays in France.)

1879. February.*" Look here, upon this Picture and on this." (re the Closet scene in Hamlet.) (An Actor's Notes, &c. No. 3.), by Henry Irving.
(Regarding the question of *mental* portraits, or actual pictures: Mr. Irving advocating *mental portraits*.)

1880. February. " An Eye-witness of John Kemble," by Theodore Martin.
(Gives a most interesting *resumé* of Dr. Ludwig Tieck's views upon John Kemble's acting of Shakespearean and other characters, whom he saw at the Covent Garden Theatre, in that actor's farewell performances in the Spring of 1817. The strictures of Dr. Tieck, in his London letters, upon some of Kemble's imperson-ations, might, in the opinion of Mr. Theodore Martin, have been modified or not given, if he had seen Kemble in his best days. The acting of contemporary actors is also commented upon.)

„ May. *" The Pound of Flesh," by Moncure D. Conway.
(Treats of the transformation of the early farcical repre-sentation of Shylock into a character filled with pathos. He says "no one can carefully compare his Shylock with the Barabas of his contemporary [Marlowe's *Jew of Malta*], without recognising a purpose to modify and soften the popular feeling towards the Jew, to picture a man where Marlowe had painted a monster, if not indeed to mirror for Christians their own in-justice and cruelty." He then enters upon a learned and valuable account of the *Bond* story, in the Folk-tales of Persia and India, and in Semitic legendary lore.)

"The Gentleman's Magazine."

1868. Nov. " Falstaff," by Walter Maynard.
(A slight sketch of the views of Warburton, Steevens, Malone, and Ritson, upon the question of the identity of Falstaff and Sir John Oldcastle, which leads up to a favourable criticism of Mr. Mark Lemon's reading and representation of the character of *Falstaff*.)

1873. June. *" Shakespeare's Philosophers & Jesters." *Art. iv., Shakespeare's Philosophy*, by Charles Cowden Clarke.
(The volume for this year contains the preceding articles on this subject; the article here mentioned forms the last, and is a very careful analysis of the poet's philo-sophy, given through the medium of his characters.)

1877. January. *" True Story of Romeo and Juliet," by G. E. Mackay.
(An account of the Italian story of *Romeo and Juliet*, showing the discrepancies between that and Shakes-peare's version. The writer does not say which he believes to be the true version.)

„ March. *" Colley Cibber *versus* Shakespeare," by B. Barker.
(Describes the alterations made by Colley Cibber, of Shakespeare's plays:—*King John* [re-christened "Papal Tyranny"]; *Richard II*; *Richard III*; *Henry IV*; *Henry V*; and *Henry VI*. Also criticises favourably Mr. Henry Irving's revival of *Richard III*.)

1878. March. *"Shakespeare's Sonnets," by T. A. Spalding.
(The writer says, his "main object is to show that the first hundred and twenty-six sonnets, at any rate, are arranged, in the quarto of 1609, in an order that is probably chronological." That "the first hundred and twenty-six sonnets were addressed by Shakspere to a friend who is unknown, but whose christian name was probably the same as the poet's, during a somewhat lengthened period, possibly about three years, and have for subject chiefly the phases through which the friendship passed." He adopts the method of treatment of Gervinus, and rejects that of Mr. Gerald Massey. The article is exhaustive, and the treatment æsthetic.)

,,   April.   "At Stratford-on-Avon." (Anon.)
(A sketch.)

1879. August. *"Notes on the Historic Play of 'Edward III.'" Part 1, by A. C. Swinburne.

,,   Sept.   *Ditto, Part 2, by A. C. Swinburne.
(These articles form a most valuable contribution to Shakespearean criticism, and contain an admirable analysis of this play. The writer concludes:—"For myself, I am, and have always been, perfectly satisfied with one single and simple piece of evidence that Shakespeare had not a finger in the concoction of King Edward III. He was the author of King Henry V.")

1880. February.*"The Original of Shylock," by S. L. Lee.
(An ingenious attempt to fix the identity of Shylock with one named Lopez, "who came into considerable prominence, while the dramatist was growing up to manhood, and was treated with great indignity because of his religious belief towards the end of his remarkable career, which closed only a few months before The Merchant of Venice appeared." Lopez was hanged at Tyburn in 1593.)

"Fraser's Magazine."

1877. Jan.   *"The Teutonic Tree of Existence," by Dr. Karl Blind.
(Derives [at page 108] Shakespeare's Weird Sisters of Macbeth, from one of the Nornes, Urd or Wurd—signifying Past. A very learned and carefully written article.)

June.   *"An old German Poem and a Vedic Hymn," by Dr. Karl Blind.
(Points out the striking use of Alliteration in Macbeth, and derivation of the Weird Sisters from the Germanic Norns.")

,,   Nov.   *"What Shakespeare learnt at School," by Prof. T. S. Baynes."
(A conjectural account of Shakespeare's schoolhood.)

1880. January. "What Shakespeare learnt at School." Art: II, by Prof: T. S. Baynes.
(Continued.)

,,   May.   *Ditto, Art: III., by Prof. T. S. Baynes.
(Continued. These articles show great research and keen criticism of the author, and should be carefully perused. There must necessarily be an element of conjecture in the consideration of the question propounded. In the first article, Prof. Baynes says, "I purpose gathering together some indirect points of evidence bearing on the subject [of Shakespeare's

learning], that have hitherto been overlooked. The question of Shakespeare's classical quotations is a large one, and in dealing with it, I hope to throw some further light on the sources he employed, as well as on his method of using them."

In the *second* article, the writer says, after drawing a comparison with Ovid:—"It is clear therefore, I think, that Shakespeare not only studied the 'Metamorphoses' in the original, but that he read the different stories with a quick and open eye for any name, incident, or allusion that might be available for use in his own dramatic labours."

The *third* article is mainly concerned with a further consideration of the dramatist's indebtedness to Ovid, and the influence the study of that poet had over him. Virgil is also instanced. Upon which the writer says:— "it is in the poetical treatment [in allusion to *Lucrece*] of these facts that Shakespeare's obligation to Ovid are most apparent." . . . . . "but after the proofs I have given, it will hardly, I think, be denied that Shakespeare was quite capable of studying the celebrated Roman story [of *Lucrece*] in the original sources, and that he certainly did so in relation to Ovid's version of it." . . . . . " And though I must defer for the present the wider evidence of his Roman studies, and especially of his familiarity with Ovid, which I have collected from a careful examination of the dramas, enough perhaps has been already adduced to illustrate the main position of these papers, that Shakespeare was a fair Latin scholar, and in his earlier life a diligent student of Ovid.")

"The Fortnightly Review."

1870. Jan. *" Christopher Marlowe, by Professor E. Dowden.
(A most valuable article upon this dramatist, and should be read, as he and Shakespeare were " the two foremost men of the Elizabethan artistic movement.")

1871. Feb. *" Old Criticisms on Old Plays and Players," by the Hon. R. Lytton.
(An interesting account of Georg Christian Lichtenberg's visit to London in 1775, and of his graphic description of Garrick, whom he saw in the character of Hamlet at Drury Lane Theatre, and his opinions upon Garrick's interpretation.)

1873. March. *" The Historical Element in Shakspeare's 'Falstaff,' " by James Gairdner.
(Gives an account of the lives of *Sir John Oldcastle* and *Sir John Fastolf*. Says: "the purpose served by the introduction of Sir John Falstaff into the play [*Henry IV.*] is clearly an artistic one; Sir John was necessary to set forth the dissolute life of the young prince, and to show the influences by which he was supposed to be led away. From this point of view the character may be acknowledged as altogether mythical, and yet the aim of its creation was historical;" and concludes, "and now I hope it has been shown that the Falstaff of Shakspeare, much as it undoubtedly owed to the rich imagination of and incomparable wit of the dramatist, was an embodiment of traditions respecting two distinct historical personages—traditions largely tinged with prejudice, but still not unworthy to be considered as reflecting the opinions of the age, and preserving, at the same time, some little details of genuine historic fact which, if they had not been stereotyped by genius, would by this time have perished irrecoverably.")

1875. January. *" King Lear," by J. W. Hales.
(Begins with an historical consideration of this play, and follows on to an exposition of the ethical elements embodied in the characters of *Lear* and *Cordelia*.)

,, May. *" The Three Stages of Shakespeare," by A. C Swinburne.

1876. May. *Do., continued.
(These two essays contain a masterly analysis of the works of the dramatist; the author's "*Study of Shakespeare*" will however be found more accessible than these numbers, *vide* 1880, in "List of Works.")

"Macmillan's Magazine."

1868. Feb. *" Lady Macbeth," by Fanny Kemble.
(A very able defence of the position that Lady Macbeth died of *wickedness*, and not of *remorse*, and gives an analysis of her character.)

1874. Sept. *" Who Wrote our Old Plays ?" by F. G. Fleay.
(With regard to Shakespeares's works, the writer introduces the results of his *metrical* investigations, in determining the date of *Cymbeline*, and dwells upon the *external evidence* method, and says :—" *Cymbeline* was therefore written near *Macbeth* and *Lear*, and probably soon after." He raises the questions of " Who were the authors of *Henry VI.*?" " Is there, or is there not, any Shaksperian work in *The Birth of Merlin* and *Fair Em ?*" and " How do you account for the differences between the folio and quarto editions of *Richard III.*?" but does not attempt to answer them. He asks for a satisfactory answer, on "æsthetic grounds only.")

,, Dec. *" On the Extract from an Old Play in Hamlet," by F. G. Fleay.
(Says, in discussing the authorship of the "Old Play," [*Macbeth*, Act ii., sc. 2] " We may confidently assign the greater part of it to Nash, if not the whole." . . . . " I hold then that the object which Shakspere had in view, in introducing this speech into *Hamlet*, was to expose the weakness of his opponent Nash as a playwright, and to utilize a piece of work which he had lying idle by him." Of course this statement is purely *conjectural*, and indeed the whole article bristles with guesses, perhaps ingenious.)

1875. Jan. " The New Hamlet, and His Critics," by A. Templar.
(A protest, and in very plain ungarbled terms, against the fulsome laudation that greeted Mr. H. Irving upon his first performance of *Hamlet* at the Lyceum Theatre. At the same time this keen-sighted critic metes out the praise that is fairly due to this distinguished actor.)

1876. August. *" The Elder Hamlet," by George MacDonald.
(He says, " The ghost in *Hamlet* is as faithfully treated as any character in the play. Next to Hamlet himself he is to me the most interesting person of the drama." The article consists of an admirable analysis of the character of the *Ghost*, or older Hamlet.)

1878. Nov. *" Shakespeare as an Adapter," by Edward Rose.
(Upon the constructive and dramatic skill of the dramatist. " How completely Shakespeare was this [a true dramatic poet], has never, I think, been sufficiently shown, and it is an omission in criticism which can hardly be supplied in half-a-dozen pages.")

"The Reader."

1864. Nov. 19. "Miss Faucit's 'Lady Macbeth,'" by C. H.
(Discussing how part should be rendered. Upholds Miss F.'s rendering: "As a delicate, loving woman, weak-minded, cruel only in her devotion to a husband whom she worships, and too tenderly constructed to sustain the affliction of remorse, after the mischief of her criminality has been effected.")

1866. Feb. 17. *"A New Life of Shakespeare." (*Anon.*)
(An article of three columns, essentially upon the vagaries of Shakespearean critics, and deprecates any further attempt at guesswork. Takes for its theme Mr. Halliwell's announcement of "another Life of Shakespeare," and says, *in passim*:—"if Mr. Halliwell really winds up Shakespeare's life, writings and times, and by the magnitude and comprehensiveness of his work puts an end to all further attempts in that direction, anticipating and enclosing in one view everything that can be said or collected on the subject, and leaving those who come after him a barren inheritance of used-up resources, he will confer an inestimable service on our literature.")

,, July 28. "Shakespeare as a Mad Doctor." (*Anon.*)
A review of *Shakespeare's Delineations of Insanity, Imbecility, and Suicide*, by A. O. Kellog, M.D. Rightly condemns this book, and Dr. Kellog's ambitious attempt at unravelling the problem of Shakespeare's knowledge of mental diseases.)

"The Spectator."

1877. Sep. 6 & 13. "Mr. Swinburne and Shakespeare," by F. J. Furnivall.
(An attack upon Mr. Swinburne, in reference to his articles in the *Gentleman's Magazine*, on *Edward III.*, afterwards reprinted with additions of no value; *see* 1879 above, in List of Works.)

"The Saturday Review."

1876. Aug. 12. *"Shakspeare and His Adapters." (*Anon.*)
(An interesting account of the adapters of Shakespeare's plays, including Cibber, Goethe [who amended *Romeo and Juliet* for the Weimar Theatre], Otway, Dryden, Davenant, the Duke of Buckingham, and Nahum Tate.)

1878. Nov. 16. "*Minor Notices.*" Giving a stringent notice of Mr. Vaughan's book. *New Readings of Shakespeare's Tragedies.*
(Well deserved; "amazingly silly book.")

"All the Year Round."

1879. Jan. 25. *"Young Shakespeare's 'Hamlet,'" by W. K. Sawyer, F.S.A.
(A critical account of the 1603 quarto, and comparison with that of 1604. The writer is "disposed to look with doubt on surmises as to yet earlier drafts and less perfect skeletons, as also to treat with contempt the imperfect-note theory, in relation to this edition (albeit there might have been publication without consent); and so it pleases us to regard this quarto of 1603 as in effect the work of the poet's youth, or, as we call it, Young Shakespeare's Hamlet," page 141. This article is a most valuable contribution, in the elucidation of the differences between the two quarto editions.)

1880. Jan. 3. *On Troilus and Cressida (Anon).
(An account of Dryden's version of this play, entitled:
" Troilus and Cressida, or Truth found too late," 1679.)

" Belgravia."

1878. Aug. *Art: " The Falstaff of Ossian," by Standish O'Grady.
(A parallel drawn between Finn Mac Cool of Irish Romance
and the Falstaff of Shakespeare).

"The Contemporary Review."

1876. June. *" The Drama," by W. H. Pollock.
(The general view of the Early, Shakespearean and Continental Drama.)

" The Saint Paul's Magazine."

1871. Nov. *Art: " Voltaire on Hamlet," by C. E. Meetkerke.
(A short account of Voltaire's views of this play.)

"Chambers's Journal."

1864. April 23. " Shakspeare." Tercentenary Number.
(An interesting sketch of his life, &c.)

" The Standard."

1879. Feb. 1. " Readings and Renderings of Shakespeare."
(A long review of over two columns of Mr. Vaughan's
work, vide The Saturday Review, Nov. 16th, 1878. Commendatory.)

"The Evening Standard."

1880. Feb. 2. " Shylock's Prototype." (From the Cologne Gazette.)
(Gives the story of a Christian Shylock.)

" Life."

1879. July 19. Art: " Something more about Shakespeare."

" The Cornhill Magazine."

1871. Sept. *" On the Character of Cleopatra." (Anon.)
(A carefully written estimate of this character. The
writer says, and attempts to prove, " that Cleopatra
was one of the most fascinating women that ever
lived, and that Shakspeare's picture of her is quite
unexampled for its truthfulness, even in his own
wonderful gallery of portraits.")

1872. August. *" Dramatic Situation and Dramatic Character."
(Anon.)
(After a brief notice of the treatment of dramatic situation
by the poets of Ancient Greece, the writer enters upon
a critical examination of Shakespeare's treatment of
situation and character and shows his supremacy in
treatment over his contemporaries.)

1872. October. *"The Origin of Shakespeare's Tempest." (Anon.)

(The writer critically examines the hypotheses mentioned by Johannes Meissner in his *Untersuchungen über Shakespeare's Sturm* [1872], regarding the sources of this play, and the similiarity Jacob Ayrer's *Fair Sidea* bears to it. This poet died 1605. *Does not* assent to the supposition that Shakespeare borrowed from Ayrer. The writer is opposed to German subtleties, and in concluding, says:—" That in the simple portraiture of the aims, passions, and imaginations of universal human nature lies a wisdom deeper than allegory, a poetry more moving than any subtleties of metaphysical analysis.")

1876. January. "A Stage Iago," by J. R. S.

(A protest against a continuation on the stage, of a *stage* Iago, the text for which the writer takes from Macready's entry in his journal, that the gentleman he once played with, played Iago like a "creeping cat." He wishes for a representation of that character "as Shakspere made him." The real Iago, he says, "is preeminently the man of practical ability, in the exercise of which, for its own sake, he takes a pure delight, "but when he can turn his powers to a bad object, his delight is doubled. He has a great love of wickedness apart from all personal considerations.")

"The Englishman's Magazine."

1865. Nov. *"Some Peculiarities of Shakespeare's Language," by C. M. Ingleby, M.A., L.L.D.

(In the volume of this magazine for 1864 and in the one for the year herein mentioned, there are two articles upon Shakespeare, which I have not, however, read.)

"The Leisure Hour."

1871. Dec. *"Ghosts and Ghost-Lore. *Shakespeare's Ghosts*." (*Anon.*)

(A review of the chief passages of ghost-lore in his writings relating to the ghosts in *Hamlet*, *Julius Cæsar*, *Macbeth*, and those which appeared in *Richard III*, and to Richmond in the night before the battle of Bosworth Field.)

"Modern Thought."

1880. July. *"The Whitewashing of Shylock," by J. Laister.

(A calmly considered article. The position of this writer is "that Shakespeare disliked the Jews as cordially as he can be supposed to have disliked anything or anybody. This fact may add to the sum of Christian intolerance, but it leaves Shakespeare honest." He entirely opposes the views of Mr. F. Hawkins, given in *The Theatre* for Nov., 1879, and says, "Shakespeare has seldom referred to the Jews in his other plays, but wherever he has done so it has been disparagingly," and concludes by saying, "and as knavery was in fact all on his [Shylock's] side, whilst the honesty was all the other [Antonio's], our ethics as well as our creed must undergo a transformation before Shakespeare's Jew can be converted into a Hero.")

"The Era."

1876. May 7. "The Dramatic Use of the Supernatural." (*Anon.*)

(The writer *in passim* deals in a very lucid manner with Shakespeare's masterly treatment of the supernatural element, in his conceptions of ghosts and witches in his plays.)

"The Journal of the British Archæological Association."

1860. Dec. 31. Remarks by Mr. Syer Cuming upon the Discovery of a cross, in a hole, in a beam of Shakespeare's House at Stratford-upon-Avon (*vide* p. 330).
(A very curious and interesting contribution. Date of the cross ascribed to the first half of the sixteenth century. "Resembles the simple way-side crosses of the thirteenth and fourteenth centuries, and consists of a plain quadrangular shaft supported in a flat plinth, reached by four steps encompassing it on either side." The fragment measures but one inch and a quarter in height, and eight-tenths in diameter at the base.")

"The Architect."

1874. Oct. 31.
to
1875. June 26.
*A series of articles on "The Architecture and Costume of Shakspere's Plays," by Edward W. Godwin, F.S.A.
(Certainly the most valuable contributions to Shakespearean Archæology of recent date. Much profound research is manifested in regard to the periods of the plays, costumes, origin of plots, and the manner in which they should be represented on the stage, consonant with the requirements of archæology and architecture.)

1876. Oct. 14 & 21. "Archæology on the Stage," by W. Burgess.
(Essentially an attack upon Mr. Godwin's designs of costumes, etc., for Shakespeare's plays, especially for Henry V., produced at the Queen's Theatre, Oct., 1876 replied to in the following number by Mr. Godwin.)

"The British Architect."

1880. Feb. 13. *"The Costume of the Merchant of Venice," by E. W. Godwin, F.S.A.
(Numerous sketches from authorities of the sixteenth century, with an article upon the same.)

„ Mar. 26. *"Sketches of Costume for 'As You Like It,'" by E. W. Godwin, F.S.A.
(Gives numerous sketches of dresses, etc., contemporary with the period of this play. This learned antiquary purposes to include, in the succeeding numbers of this journal, articles upon all the plays of the poet, with numerous illustrations.)

"The Pall Mall Gazette."

1877. Feb. 23. "New Books and New Editions."
"(Giving a review *in passim* of *Shakespeare from an American Point of View, including an Inquiry as to his Religious Faith and his Knowledge of Law, with the Baconian Theory considered,* by George Wilkes. The reviewer speaks highly of the ingenuity of this author in working out his arguments, but condemnatory of his views, that Shakespeare was a *Roman Catholic,* and paid homage to rank, and treated with contempt the common people.)

"The Literary World."

(Four extremely interesting articles upon this play,
suggested by Mr Horace Howard Furness's edition of
King Lear, forming Vol. V. of his "New Variorum
Edition of Shakespeare." Professor Bayne opens the
first article of this *Occasional Study* by saying, "It is
not my purpose to criticise Dr. Furness's *Lear*, but to
make the appearance of his edition an occasion for
briefly considering the drama itself:" he then presents
the reader with a most carefully considered analysis
of the play, preceded by a few remarks upon the "able
and brilliant opinions" of Hazlitt and Shelley. For
clearness of style and masterly treatment, Professor
Bayne's four articles may be ranked amongst the
most important contributions to Shakespearean Study.
We are promised another article from the pen of this
scholar, which will probably conclude this *Study*.)

"The Globe." (*Newspaper.*)

(A short *leader*, suggested by a paper read on the
"Stratford" Portrait, at a recent meeting of the
Birmingham Press Club. The author's name is not
given. The gist of the communication, according to
the *Globe* writer is as follows:—"The author gave an
account of the circumstances under which, about
twenty years ago, the picture was found stowed away
on an upper landing in the residence of Mr. Hunt, the
Town Clerk of Stratford. It was a dilapidated canvas,
on which was dimly visible the rough, coarse portrait
of a man with a large beard and moustache, and with
the face nearly covered with hair. A picture-restorer,
then engaged by the Corporation to restore the pictures
in the Guildhall, was at once appealed to. The hair,
beard, and moustache speedily yielded to his solvents,
and lo! under the first portrait appeared another, with
a dress closely resembling the bust in the church from
which the same restorer had recently removed the coat
of white paint, applied at the suggestion of Malone,
and substituting the original colours. So near was
the resemblance between the bust and the picture,
especially in the dress, that it became a question
which was the original. But the fellow-townsmen of
the deceased bard had no doubt that the portrait was
that of Shakespeare, and they treasure the canvas as
such. The *Athenæum* at the time described it as a
modern daub, possibly a tavern sign 'Shakespeare's
Head.' Were we even to discover that the *Athenæum*
was right, the now famous 'Stratford' Shakespeare
would still be valued. Mr. Hunt was offered £1,000 for
it when it left the hands of the restorer.")

NOTE.—This attempt is merely tentative, but it is hoped, that
sufficient has been here recorded to guide the student.

APPENDIX.

In consequence of having suffered from ill-health, since this work was announced for publication last April, an enforced delay has deferred its issue until now. The proof sheets up to May, have been ready for the press for some months; but waiting complete restoration of my working powers, matter has grown so rapidly in regard to Shakespearean literature, that I have found it necessary, and indeed it is due to my subscribers, to bring the principal references down to date, and incorporate them where possible in the body of the book, and the rest to form an *Appendix;* which may not be unacceptable to students of Shakespeare. By an oversight, in compiling the Selected Articles &c. from the *Athenæum,* an important communication has been omitted, which appeared in that journal of the 30th April, 1864. [1] It refers to the valuable discovery made by Mr. J. O. Halliwell, and communicated by him, that Shakespeare had not retired from the King's Company on March 15th, 1604. This fact is embedded, says Mr. Halliwell, "in a large folio manuscript volume which has been kindly confided to the care of the Rev. T. Granville, the respected vicar of Stratford-on-Avon, by the authorities of the Lord Chamberlaine's Office, and is now being publicly exhibited for a time by their permission at the Birth-place in Henley Street. It contains a minute account of the expenses incurred for the materials of the dresses for those who took part in the procession at the visit of King James the First, to the City of London in the year 1604; and amongst the entries is one to the effect that our great dramatist was furnished with four and a half yards of 'skarlet red cloth' on the occasion." The title of this volume is then given, followed by an extract containing the names of the King's Player's, and the quantities of red cloth apportioned to each, that of Shakespeare heading the list thus:—" William Shakespeare, iiij yardes, Skarlet red cloth, di." After a lapse of over sixteen years, the following paragraph appeared in the *Athenæum* (June 19, 1880.)

---

[1] With regard to the articles and correspondence in the *Athenæum* and *Notes and Queries,* it has not been considered necessary to extend backwards the references to the *first* numbers; although, for a purely bibliographical purpose, such would be invaluable.

"The extreme rarity of contemporary manuscript notices of Shakspeare is exemplified by the singular circumstance that not even a trivial one has yet been unearthed by the extensive and well-directed researches of the Historical Commission. The New Shakspere Society has to tell the same tale. In the last number of its *Transactions*, just issued, is a copy of a manuscript respecting the delivery of red cloth to Shakspeare on the occasion of the procession of James I. through London in 1604. It appears as a novelty, with an interesting note by Mr. Furnivall, but the document itself was printed in the *Athenæum* many years ago (April 30th, 1864), long before the Society was founded."

This, as most readers would expect, was followed by an explanation from Mr. F. J. Furnivall the director of the *New Shakspere Society*, and as it tells its own story best, I have extracted it, with the Editor's comments thereon. (*Athenæum*, June 26th, 1880.)

"Mr. Furnivall sends us a long explanation of the appearance of the MS. relating to Shakspeare's four and a half yards of red cloth in the *Transactions* of the New Shakspere Society; he declares it does not appear in the *Transactions:*—

'It appears in one of our "Appendices," which I hoped all workers knew have from the first been devoted almost only to reprints and reviews. Before it stands a reprint of the only three leaves left of William Wager's "Cruell Debtter," 1566; after it, the reprint of Prof. Wilson's "Solution of the Mystery of Doubletime in Shakspeare." My note 2 on p. 11* of the Appendix refers to my "Leopold Shakspere Introduction," p. cvii. where I name two of the places where the red cloth business has been mentioned: ".Athenæum, April 30th, 1864; Dyce. viii, 473" (second edition). To represent me, then, as reproducing a notorious old thing "as a novelty" is rather a joke. The thing is so entirely an *a b c* matter to working students of Shakspere that the need of renaming its first printer on every occasion no more occurred to me than the like need did when I printed Dr. Forman's "Book of Plays" from Ashm. MS. 208 in our Appendix for 1875-6. (By accident I in this put a "Richard II." down to Shakspere which the description of it shows cannot possibly be his.) And as my friend Mr. Walford D. Selly—at my request, if I remember right—copied the document from the Lord Chamberlain's Records, they, and not the *Athenæum*, were quoted as the authority for the document. Had I meant to claim the thing as a novelty, it would of course have been put in the body of our *Transactions*, with the novelty from the Record Office that (by Mr. G. H. Overend's kindness) does appear there, namely, the very curious "Bill of Complaint of George Maller, glazier and trainer of players to Henry VIII., against Thomas Arthur, tailor, his pupil," which throws such an interesting light on the state of the profession, if so it might be called, in Henry VIII.'s days. Perhaps I may be excused for saying that in the same volume and our other publications is evidence that we are fairly up to our work, though we may pay other students the compliment of knowing as much as we do, or much more.'"

The Editor thus remarks:—

"The distinction between the *Transactions* and the Appendixes is too subtle for us, and any ordinary scholar would suppose, from the way in which it is printed, that Mr. Furnivall regards this MS. as a novelty. However, Mr. Furnivall's letter simply confirms what we said: that nothing new appears to turn up about Shakspeare."

Another omission is the following:—

1880. *Jan. 31.   (*Athenæum*.)   *A Study of Shakspeare*, by A. C. Swinburne. *Memoranda on the Tragedy of Hamlet*, by J. O. Halliwell-Phillipps, F.R.S.

> A long and critical review of these works. Opens with pointing out an inconsistency in Mr. Swinburne's treatment of his subject. The author says: "Having from well nigh the first years I can remember made the study of Shakespeare the chief intellectual business and found in it the chief spiritual delight of my whole life. I can hardly think myself less qualified than another to offer an opinion on the metrical points at issue." "It is not, so to speak, the literal but the spiritual order which I have studied to observe and to indicate: the periods which I seek to define belong not to chronology but to art." The reviewer says: "Surely the attempt to evolve a spiritual order is no less hopeless. He who thinks that Shakspeare wrote plays to bring out his thoughts and emotions as they arose little understands Shakspeare's character or his life." Mr. Swinburne receives however a not too adequate praise for the subtlety of his remarks, his analytical power, and the manifestation of "that variety of sympathy which is the first requisite in any man who would write about most various of poets and of men." After discussing the alleged influence of Rabelais upon the dramatist, and showing that "as big as Gargantua's mouth" [in *As You Like It*.] is not a reference to Rabelais but the "'History of Gargantua,' probably printed in England as early as 1575;" Mr. Halliwell-Phillipps's work is examined, and the reviewer says, that as regards the character of Hamlet. "There can be no doubt that Mr. Swinburne is right in his estimate of Hamlet's character, and Mr. Halliwell-Phillipps, we are glad to see, takes the same view." The whole article should be carefully read.)

The foregoing omissions, I trust will be duly noted, as they include the record of one more controversy in the Shakespearean arena. Not that the student cannot dispense with such trifles, but it may tend to show him, how useless it is to lose one's equanimity of temper, over such small errors, whilst there are weightier subjects at hand, requiring elucidation. Further, it may bring once more to his mind the fact, that no one man has an exclusive right to Shakespeare.

The addittional selections I wish to make from THE ATHENÆUM are as follows:—

1880.   June 12.   "The Philosophy of Hamlet," by Thomas Tytler, M.A.

> (A review of this remarkable book. The reviewer very properly and justly says:—"The whole pamphlet—for it is little more—affords a curious instance of the darkening of the perceptions that may result from the study of the letter and the neglect of the spirit, and is enough to justify the heresy that Shakspearean commentators do more to confuse their readers than to aid them.")

1880.   July 17.*   "King Lear."   Edited by Horace Howard Furness, Ph.D.

> (A review of Vol. V. of *A New Variorum Edition of Shakespeare*. Speaks very highly of Dr. Furness' work, and considers his partial adoption of the old spelling. The reviewer differs from Dr. Furness, whose advocacy of the old spelling, he bases upon the ground that we do

not modernize Spenser; and asserts that Spenser's phraseology is intentionally archaic. "With a deliberate purpose" he says "he [Spenser] stuffs his text with archaisms, and he affects a style of spelling which is a portion of his method in art." On the other hand, there is no proof that Shakespeare corrected his manuscripts, and supervised the printing of his plays, and "the spelling, then, of that edition which is held to possess most authority, the first folio, is that either of Heminge and Condell, by whom it was given to the world, or more probably by the printers.")

1883.	July 24.	"The Melancholy Jaques," by Oswald Crawford.

(Upon the pronunciation of *Jaques* in *As You Like It*. Objects to its being pronounced "Jaikes" or "Jaikwes" and advocates the French pronunciation.)

,,	July 31.	Ditto, by Grant Allen.

(After giving several extracts from the dramatists' plays, this writer says, "On the whole, therefore, I incline to think that Shakspeare pronounced the name as if written in modern English 'Jah-kez,' the final *e* being distinctly articulated."

,,	Ibid.	Ditto, by Dr. B. Nicholson.

(Inclines to a variable pronunciation according to scansion. In four instances, "Jā | qués," and in two, "it might read Jāqués.")

,,	Aug. 14.	Ditto, by Oswald Crawford.

(Merely differs from some of the statements made by Mr. Grant Allen, and holds to his original view.)

,,	Ibid.	Ditto, by Frank A. Marshall.

(Says "Jaques, must be a dissyllable, but need it assume the horrible form of 'Jai-quez' or 'Jaikwes'? Why not preserve the essentially French character of the name, and pronounce it 'Jāhk-es'? I put the *ah* to represent the French *a*.")

,,	Aug. 21.	Ditto, by Grant Allen.

(A reply to Mr. Oswald Crawford. After a lame attempt at sarcasm, which sensible readers will pass by, this writer says "'Jaques' in Shakspeare being scanned as two syllables must be so pronounced, when it occurs at the end of a line as well as when it occurs in the middle.")

,,	Ibid.	Ditto, by J. T.

(Quotes a sonnet of Mr. Alfred Tennyson, the Poet Laureate, to show that he "gives a dissyllabic value to the name of the Shakspearean Jaques." The line italicised is:— "*Our kindlier, trustier Jacques, past away.*")

,,	Aug. 23.*	"The First Two Editions of Romeo and Juliet," by James Spedding.

(Discusses the differences between these two editions, and says:—"Having carefully examined all the passages referred to by Mr. Daniel, both in his introduction to the 'Parallel Texts' [Published for the *New Shakspere Society* in 1874] and in his notes to the 'revised edition' of the second quarto (1875), as proving that both quartos were 'derived from the same source,' by which I understand him to mean the same play in the same condition, I cannot think that the case is made out. I still think that the more obvious assumption was the more probable one, that the quarto of 1597 represents (printers' and transcribers' errors allowed for) the the play as originally produced, and that the quarto of 1599 represents (subject to a similar and rather larger allowance for such errors) a second edition, printed not only from a better copy, but from a copy 'newly corrected, augmented, and amended,' as set forth in the title." Mr. Spedding then goes on to expose the guesswork of Mr. Fleay, in ascribing the first draft of this play to *G. Peele*.)

1830. *Ibid.* *Shakespeare Memoranda. Memoranda on Love's Labour's Lost, King John, Othello, and on Romeo and Juliet, by J. O. Halliwell-Phillipps, F.R.S.*
(A review of this valuable work, (which unfortunately for the student, is *privately printed*), and commendatory.)

,, Sept. 4. "The Melancholy Jaques," by Oswald Crawford.
(Returns to this discussion by a counter reply to Mr. Grant Allen, and of course remains unchanged in opinion. He believes that stage tradition is right in making one syllable of this name.)

,, *Ibid.* Ditto, by Dr. B. Nicholson.
(Says:—"Though I could once speak French with an unusually small modicum of the 'accent Britannique,' I yet naturally pronounced Shakspeare's word, 'Jai-ques.'")

,, *Ibid.* Ditto, by T. Standish Haly.
(Informs his readers through the editor, that he "was horrified, on a recent visit to Drury Lane, to hear my old friend called 'Jä-quēs'"! And says:—"that Jacques is a common surname at Stratford-on-Avon and in the surrounding district." The remainder of this letter consists of useless guesswork.)

,, *Ibid.* Ditto, by A. B. G.
(Upon the "syllabic force of *e* mute in the works of the French Poets." Of no value or consequence.)
[The Editor very properly appends the notice:—"We cannot insert any more letters on this subject."]

,, Sept. 11. "The Date of Shakspeare's Fifty-Fifth Sonnet," by Thomas Tyler.
(Differs from some critics in regard to the date of this Sonnet, and arrives at the conclusion, that "there can be little doubt, that the fifty-fifth sonnet was written after the publication of the 'Palladis Tamia' in 1598. We must therefore conclude that those critics are in error who infer, from the mention in this same book of Meres's of Shakspeare's 'sugred Sonnets among his private friends,' that the whole of the sonnets collected and printed in 1609 already (in 1598) existed in manuscript. To the fifty-fifth sonnet I should assign the approximate date of 1599.")

,, Oct. 2. *Hamlet, Prince of Denmark:: Tragedie en Cinq Actes de William Shakespeare.* Traduite en Prose et en Vers par Theodore Reinach."
(A review of this translation, wherein M. Reinach's successes in difficult passages are very highly spoken of. Of the work the reviewer says "It is inferior to none in correctness, and it shows not only in the rendering of the text, but in the prefatory matter and in the choice of notes, taste and judgment together with a close and intimate knowledge of the subject." Some very interesting examples of M. Reinach's treatment are given.)

"The Academy."

1880. June 5. In *Notes and News* Column, an announcement that "Max Wolff, has published, at J. Hörning's Heidelberg, his inaugural dissertation for his doctor's degree on · John Ford, an Imitator of Shakspere.'"

„ June 12. "Shakspere in Old Spelling," by F. J. Furnivall.
(A copy of a proposal, sent by Mr. Furnivall, to the members of the New Shakspere Society, for an edition of Shakespeare's work in *Old Spelling*. He enters very fully into the reasons for reprinting the texts in the spelling of the dramatist's time.")

„ *Ibid.* In *Notes and News* Column, in reference to The Harness Prize Essays on the First Quarto of *Hamlet*, by Mr. C. H. Herford, and Mr. Widgery.
(It says:—"Both writers hold that the first quarto represents Shakspere's first sketch of his play. Mr. Herford's argument is founded on the differences in the leading characters in the first quarto and their full development in the second, also on the higher poetic qualities of the completed plays.")

„ June 26. In *Notes and News* Column, a brief outline of Mr. F. J. Furnivall's *Forewords* in Mr. Griggs's *facsimile* of the second quarto of *Hamlet*, 1604.
(Points out, that he "shows how much more important for the character of Hamlet and the play the second quarto is than the first folio.")

„ *Ibid.* "Mr. Swinburne and Fletcher's Share in Henry VIII," by Mr. F. J. Furnivall.
(One more attack upon Mr. Swinburne, by this controversalist. He opens with:—"Some of your readers may remember that in 1876, Mr. Swinburne stated that there were no triple endings in Fletcher's part of his and Shakspere's *Henry VIII.*, and that therefore the part assigned to Fletcher by Mr. Spedding and Mr. Tennyson could not be his. I at once pointed out, what most people knew, that there were some *thirty* triple endings in the Fletcher part of *Henry VIII.*, and I gave a list of them." Mr. Furnivall then proceeds by citing twenty words, and stating how many times some of them recur. This letter contains some very curious remarks; such as "Mr. Swinburne saw he was beaten and must change his ground, though he did admit the fact in words." He says, Mr. Swinburne's argument is "*absolutely worthless.*" "Evidently just the same recklessness that Mr. Swinburne had displayed in the *Edward II.*, article about Shakspere's words—I made him admit that he was wrong in five instances out of seven—Mr. Swinburne had shown again in his argument about *Henry VIII.*" "A more crude and contradictory theory of the structure of *Henry VIII.* than that which Mr. Swinburne has put forth I never saw." The general tone of this communication, cannot be very gratifying to every humble student, and less so to those learned critics of Shakespeare, who are too modest to style themselves *scholars*. In the *Academy*, of the 3rd of July, Mr. Swinburne thus closes his share in this tedious if not profitless controversy:—

, July 3. "MR. SWINBURNE writes under date of June 26, 1880:— "A correspondent of yours affirms in your issue of this morning that I have 'never answered' a 'challenge' put forward 'in an early number of the *Academy* of this year.' Certainly I have not done so. And most assuredly I shall not.

"The person in question has perfectly succeeded in his evident and elaborate endeavour to put himself outside the pale of possible intercourse. With such a person I should almost as soon think of entering into correspondence as of entering into controversy. He is absolutely free and absolutely welcome to say, to write, and to print anything about me he may please. But he must not hope—and he need not fear—ever again to attract even as much notice as this from the hand of your obedient Servant, ALGERNON CHARLES SWINBURNE.")

1880. July 10. "Fletcher's and Shakspere's Triple Endings," by F. J. Furnivall.

(He says, "I have this week to ask whether all Fletcher's plays contain that 'perpetual predominance of triple terminations so peculiarly and notably dear to that poet' which Mr. Swinburne puts forward as the metrical test of Fletcher's work. As my object is to compare their proportion in Fletcher's plays with that in his part of *Henry VIII.*, I take the same number of lines in that part from his two plays—*The Knight of Malta* and *The Little French Lawyer*." After elaborating his views, and citing several words from these plays, and twenty-four lines from some of Shakespeare's, besides three from Milton, he says:—"Having thus shown that Mr. Swinburne's attack on the positions of Mr. Spedding, Mr. Tennyson, Mr. Browning, Profs. Dowden and Ingram, and myself, with regard to Fletcher's share in *Henry VIII.*, and his triple endings, though brought forward with great pretence of knowledge, and many sneers against us, has failed in every point, I will, with your leave, proceed to enter my protest against another 'flat burglary' committed on Shakspere by *men far worthier of respect in the Shakspere field.*" The words italicised may be considered worth remembering by those who are interested in the good taste occasionally displayed by ripe Shakespearean scholars.)

  „   July 17. In *Notes and News* column, a paragraph stating that Dr. Tanger of Berlin, has "made an exhaustive analysis and comparison of the first quarto of *Hamlet*, 1603, with the second quarto and first folio, after the model of Mommsen's well known study of the first quarto of *Romeo and Juliet*, 1597, with its second quarto, 1599, and the folio. And as Mommsen arrived at the conclusion that his *Romeo and Juliet* Qo.1., was grounded solely on its Qo.II., so Dr. Tanger decides that in *Hamlet*, Qo.I., there is but a misrepresentation of Qo.II."

  „   Ibid   Ditto—The next paragraph of Shakespearean interest, is in relation to the spelling of the poet's name. As it will not admit of condensing, it is here given in its entirety :—

("The last contribution to the controversy about the spelling of Shakspere's name is a note by Mr Furnivall in his Forewords to Mr. Griggs's *facsimile* of the second quarto of *Hamlet*, 1604. It has been asserted that the *f* of Shakspere's third signature to his will is the well-known and accepted contraction for *es*. There cannot be a doubt on this point," Mr. Furnivall contradicts this statement, and says :—

"As, in the second signature to his will, Shakspere ran his *k* into his long straight f, and made a looped top to it, so in his third signature he ran his *k* into his long

curved which he used in the signature to his Blackfriars mortgage, and made it look, to hasty or un-
trained man, something like one of the forms of the
contraction for final es."
We are not surprised to hear that one of the highest
M.S. authorities in London has also declared this third
—Wolf to be contradiction.")

1880. July 24. In *Notes and News* Column, in announcing the
publication of Mr. Griggs's *facsimile* of the
first two quartos, by Fisher and by Roberts, of
Shakespeare's *Midsummer Night's Dream*, 1600,
says, that Mr. Ebsworth shows,—on the question
of which quarto was before the other,—"that
the Cambridge editors were right when, in 1863,
they declared Fisher's quarto to have preceded
Roberts."

  ,,   Aug. 7. "Is the character of Hamlet, Shakspere's
Creation or not?" by F. J. Furnivall.
(An attack upon the Cambridge Editors' theory of the
first quarto of Hamlet, 1603, put forth in the Preface to
the larned Press edition of the play, "dated December 1871." The Editors maintain that Shakespeare
remodelled the old play in the year 1602, and fitted it
for the stage. That the first quarto (1603) represents
the first draft incompleted, and that there is hardly a
trace of the dramatist's hand in the first, third and
forth scenes of Act III. Mr. Furnivall after pleading
for the ael put on of what has been stigmatised "sign-
post" criticism, says:—"Depend on it that no other
mind than his conceived Hamlet's continual delays and
excuses; Claudius on his knees before an offended
God; Hamlet's resolve not to kill him; Hamlet's pulse-
proof and his Company of politic worms; Ophelia's
madness and songs; her rosemary, rue and Valentine's
Day; her dry wooing and burial; the gravediggers and
their jokes; Hamlet with the skull of Yorick; Osric's
courtiers; Hamlet's foreboding of ill; and the
manner of his revenge and death. Rest assured that
the play of Hamlet and the character of Hamlet, in the
misreputing First Quarto as well as the Second, are
what 'signpost criticism' and common sense have
always declared them to be—no old-play writer's, but
in all essentials Shakspere's own.")

  ,,   Sept 18. "On *shun*, Final, in Shakspere by F. J. Furnivall,
(Merely showing that Shakespeare's use of this termination
as *trisyllables*, does not on the whole die out in his
later plays.)

  ,,   Oct 2. In *Notes and News*, Column, an announcement
that Mr. Harold Littledale, has finished his
Introduction to the *Two Noble Kinsmen*, and
has noted some rather striking instances of
identity of thought and treatment in the
Fletcher parts of the *Two Noble Kinsmen*, and
Henry VIII." In this paragraph also is a
statement that Mr. G. Rose, "when lately
examining *Henry VIII*, from his time side,
found that the two great confusions of time in
the play were due to Fletcher, while on coming
to Shakspere's work again, there he was with
his 'to-morrow morning,' thus carrying on his
scheme of dramatic time from his earlier
scenes."

In the *selections* I have made from *Notes and Queries*, it will be noticed, that the issues of that invaluable journal for 1875, are omitted; the reason for which is, that the guesses of correspondents which fill those numbers, would take up too much of my already exhausted space, to record in detail, and it is difficult for a small hand-book of this description, to know at times which to select for the beginner's aid. Here and there, however, will be found some interesting contributions that may well be perused in their entirety. In reference to the communication to *Notes and Queries*, of March 13th, 1880, by Mr. W. F. Prideaux on "The Legend of Zarqa," as possibly being the progenitor of the legend of Birnam Wood and Dunsinane (in *Macbeth*), The Reverend Walter W. Skeat sent an extract from the *Romance of Alexander*, containing a similar story. This appeared in the issue of May 29th. He says:—

"Readers of Macbeth should note that the story of the moving wood occurs in the *Romance of Alexander*:—

"Interea Alexander. amoto. exercitu. appropinquauit se ciuitati Perses, in qua Darius consistebat: Ita vt sublimia loca montium que erant supra ipsam ciuitatem conspiciebat. Alexander autem precepit militibus suis vt inciderent ramos arborum et herbas euellerent, easque inferrent equorum pedibus et mulorum: quos videntes [printed *ridentis*] Perses ab excelsis montibus stupebant."—*Historia Alexandri magni de preliis*, ed. 1490, fol. 26.

The Middle-English version (1450 has:—

"With that commaunds he his knightis to cutte dune belyue

Powis of buskis and of braunches of bolis and of lyndis," &c.

WALTER W. SKEAT."

The other *selections* that may be added to the list are as follows:—

"Notes and Queries."

frustrate those efforts and confound orthography."
Further on he says:—" I am merely stating the result
of very careful study when I assert that there exists
no edition of any work of Shakspeare's, whether in
quarto or in folio, that is printed in any orthography
of the period." "To the critic, as Dr. Nicholson says,
the slavish reproduction of the very letters of words in
the early editions is most important, but we have such
reprints in abundance." In conclusion this writer
observes:—" the projected edition in old spelling is, in
my judgment, a work of supererogation, and a costly
luxury which, in view of more pressing work, the New
Shakspere Society may well dispense with.")

1880.   *Ibid.*   Ditto, by F. J. Furnivall.
(A rejoinder to Dr. Nicholson's remarks and says *in passim,*
"Having founded the New Shakspere Society on my
own lines, and directed it since its foundation, I claim
to be a better judge of what it was meant to do, than
Dr. Nicholson. I also claim that the rightness of
having an edition of Shakspere in the spelling of his
time is acknowledged by every ' English scholar,' as I
understand that term.")

,,   *Ibid.*   Ditto, by R. M. Spence, M.A.
(Supports Mr. Furnivall.)

,,   July 17.   Ditto, by F. J. Furnivall.)
(Merely an attack upon those who have the temerity to
disagree with Mr. Furnivall's idea upon this subject.
The Editor very wisely remarks, " This discussion is
now closed.")

,,   Aug 21.   " Shakespeariana," by R. M. Spence, M.A.
(On "The Obeli of the Globe Edition in King Henry VIII."
Suggests emendations, with guesses, to overcome the
difficulties indicated.)

,,   *Ibid.*   " Cain's Jaw-Bone," by Walter W. Skeat.
(Takes the passage "As if it were Cain's jaw-bone, that
did the first murder," in Hamlet, V. i., and elucidates
it by a quotation from Kemble's edition of *Soloman and
Saturn:*—" Tell me, why stones are not fruitful? I
tell thee, because Abel's blood fell upon a stone when
Chain [Cain], his brother slew him with the jaw-bone
of an Ass." " Hence" says Mr. Skeat " the jaw-bone
was not Cain's *own*.")

,,   *Ibid.*   " Julius Cæsar, I. iii. 128, 129, by R. R.
(One more attempt at explaining *Favors.* Suggests alteration to " Is *Ferreous*.")

,,   *Ibid.*   " King Lear," Edited by Horace H. Furness.
(A commendatory review of this edition.)

,,   Aug 28.   " Shakespeariana." " As if it were Cain's Jaw-
Bone," *Hamlet* v. i., by R. R.
(This writer says, he has a Bible printed by Day and
Serres, in 1594, with a woodcut representing Cain
about to strike Abel with a jaw-bone with teeth in it.)

,,   *Ibid*   Ditto, by K. P. D. E.
(Mentions that in one of the *Townley Mysteries,*—the
"Mactacio Abel"—" Cain is represented as having
slain his brother with a choke bon.")

,,   *Ibid*   " Romeo and Juliet," viii. 114-5, by C. F. H.
(Says " Romeo's meaning seems to be that his kiss is a
token of the final and complete dedication of himself to
to the grave." Comments also upon *Seal Engrossing*
and *dateless,* as being legal terms.)

1880. Sept. 11   In the *Miscellaneous* part, there is an announcement, that Dr. Charles Mackay is shortly to publish a work on "Obscure Words and Phrases in Shakspeare and the Elizabethan Dramatists, explained for the First Time from the Celtic Sources of the English Language and the Vernacular Idiom of the English in the Sixteenth and Seventeenth Centuries." In the year 1855 was published a pamphlet entitled "On Celtic Words used by English Writers," by the Rev. John Davies, M.A., which Dr. Mackay, may be acquainted with. It ought to be quoted in his work.

„   Sept. 25   "Shakspeariana," "Romeo and Juliet," viii. 114–15, by F. C, Birkbeck Terry.
(Merely guesswork. says :—" It is possible Romeo's words mean. 'he makes with Death an unconditional bargain.'")

„   Ibid.   Ditto, by B. C.
(Upon the words *engrossing*, differs from C. F. H., upon its being a law term. in this passage, and says " it is here used for the so-named common law offence of buying up the whole of any kind of merchandise to sell at an exorbitant profit.")

„   Ibid.   Ditto, by W. G.
(Upon the word *dateless*. Instances its having been used by a person, as meaning *insensible*.)

„   Ibid.   "Macbeth," v.iii. 55, by Dr. B. Nicholson.
(Continues discussion *N. and Q.* 6th S, I, 151, 209,, says :— " Will Mr. Whiston kindly allow me to make three remarks on his note." Without giving them in *extenso*, it need only be mentioned that *Cynea* is *not* evolved out of Dr. Nicholson's conciousness. "In conclusion," he says, " I am by no means wedded to *Cynea* but merely support it as at present the nearest or only proved approach to the Shakespearian corruption of *Cynic*.)

„   Ibid   "Macbeth," "Sag," by J. R. Haig.
(Continues discussion, *N. and Q.* 6th. S. 1, 251, 333, says that when a roof of an old house "seems to have given way, the answer will probably be · that the rafters have sagged a bit.")

„   October 2.   "Party for Person," by F. C. Birkbeck Terry.
(Points out that these terms were used synonymously in Shakespeare's time and cites *Antony and Cleopatre* v. ii. 246, (Globe Edition); *Hamlet.* II i. 42; and *Love's Labour's Lost* IV, ii. 138.)

Very few articles of importance, have appeared in the Monthly Publications, since the latest dates recorded in the body of this "Aid." The few that admit of notice are as follows:—

"The Gentleman's Magazine."

1880. September.*   "The Eclipse of Shakespeare," by Dutton Cook.
(Starts with the question :—" Is it altogether a false notion that the general sympathy with the merits of Shakespeare ever beat with a languid or intermittent pulse?" and follows with a most valuable review of the disfavour in which Shakespeare's works were held, from

the time of Dryden, in particular, down to the period in which Garrick produced some of the plays *restored,* and others malformed by himself and Cibber, Tate and the rest of improvers. He speaks of Macready and Phelps as having " shown more respect for the integrity of the poet than any of their more illustrious predecessors." Of John Kemble, he says," while professing extraordinary veneration for Shakespeare, garbled several of his plays, and acted in many very corrupt ones." " He, too, retained Cibber's 'Richard' and Tate's ' Lear,' with, in addition, the ' Tempest ' of Davenant and Dryden. The ' Coriolanus ' in which he appeared was a blending of Shakespeare and Thomson." He further says, that the fashion is to see " some great actor, or an actor believed by many to be great, has roused curiosity concerning his impersonation of the poet's more famous characters ; or when, under the pretext of illustrating Shakespeare, stage pageantry and spectacle have occupied the scene." This article should be attentively read.)

1880. October. * " A new study of ' Love's Labour's Lost,' " by S. L. Lee.

(A most valuable contribution to the study of Shakespeare in the light of contemporary history. He says, " It is no new matter for regret that so few attempts should have been made by commentators to do justice to the influence exerted by contemporary events on the Elizabethan dramatists : but it is certainly matter for surprise that no endeavour should have been made to trace any relationship between contemporary French affairs and *Love's Labour's Lost,* where the names of almost all the important characters are actually identical with the contemporary leaders in French politics." He gives a number of facts to establish his view, that " Shakespeare wrote this comedy with his eyes fixed, like those of his countrymen on the affairs of France.")

" The Cornhill Magazine."

„ August. " Why did Shakespeare write Tragedies ? " by J. S.

(Examines Mr Furnivall's hook-and-eye hypothesis, propounded in the introduction to the *Leopold Shakspere,* p cxix, and gives his objections in detail to several points raised in that essay, regarding the growth of Shakespeare's mind, as evinced in his works. The conclusion need only be here noted :—" To imagine him exhibiting men and women under conditions which he had not proved by trial is, according to Mr. Furnivall, to degrade him into the master of a puppet-show. To me, on the contrary, it seems certain that he could not have exhibited those conditions has he has done while he was himself subject to them ; and that whatever perturbations his spirit may have gone through, it had risen above them before he wrote his great tragedies into—the brightest heaven of *inventions* from which he could look down with pity upon all the disorders of mankind.")

" The Theatre."

„ September.* " Hamlet on Acting," by Percy Fitzgerald.

(An examination of Hamlet's *advice,* and concludes:—" We have thus gone through this valuable body of instruction, which, in the case of any actor that takes it to heart and developes it carefully, will be found profitable.")

1880. October. * "'Othello' in Paris," by Dutton Cook.

(An account of the representations of this play on the French stage, since 1830; also of the manner in which it was "improved," or tampered with, by Ducis for Talma the actor. *Iago* was dismissed; and the dagger substituted for the pillow in the murdering of Desdemona. This article is a very valuable contribution to the history of Shakespeare in France.)

"The Antiquary."

„ **August.*** "The Shakespeare Death-Mask," by Lord Ronald Gower.

(Gives a short history of the *Becker Death-Mask*; and inclines to the view " that it comes up to the very highest conception that he (speaking of an 'unprejudiced person.') has formed of his own ideal as well as from the very poor representations that have been handed down to us of what William Shakespeare looked on that April morn in 1616, when the everlasting day had cast over the dead poet's face a light not of this world.")

„ **September.*** "The Kesselstadt Minature," by Dr. C. M. Ingleby.

(An examination of the assertion, that this picture was painted from the Becker *Death-Mask*. Dr. Ingleby says "there is evidently no likeness between them. The very proportions of the two faces, to say nothing of contour and expression are discrepant." "The most probable conclusion to be drawn from the picture, [of which an illustration is given], assuming that it is the one which was in the Kesselstadt collection up to 1843, is that the original collector obtained not only Gerard Johnson's plaster mask of Shakspeare, but also an original picture of Ben Jonson lying in state."

"All the Year Round." (*The Monthly Part issued on October, 1st.*)

„ **October 30.** "Shakespeare's Traducers." (Anon.)

(A very sketchy account of some of the best known traducers of the poet. The writer cites many passages, but omits all references, so that what value his contribution may be imagined to possess, is dispelled by its want of more careful treatment and verification.)

"The Cape Monthly Magazine."

„ **July.*** "The Character of Polonius," by Agnus Mac Phail, M.A.

(A very careful analysis of the character of Polonius, and is doubly welcome, as evidencing the progress of Shakespearean Scholarship at Cape Town. The writer says in his prefaratory remarks; ".All the characters in *Hamlet* are bound with an indissoluble golden chain round the feet of the royal Dane. They tax their brains and rack them as carded wool, and yet they cannot solve the riddle of the moody Titan. They see Atlas convulsed and trembling to its very roots, and yet they cannot divine the cause of the commotion, but they keep at a distance from its frowning rocks, lest their fall might sweep them to ruin. This universal, bewildering perplexity is the occasion of Polonius." He then goes on to say, that Iago deprived of "his insatiable stomach for unadulterated mischief and callous, pernicious devilry, and he might then play the *rôle* of Polonius."

Mr. Mac Phail further says there is a family likeness
between these two characters, although Iago was not
an eaves-dropper. Unfortunately, he *in passim*, speaks
of "Shakspeare, himself entrapped into an early
marriage;" the evidence of the *entrapping* is yet
wanting. "Polonius," says the writer, "on all
occasions, advises the king as a disinterested courtier,
professing the most loyal attachment, but all his
actions beyond the circle of his family smack of a
wise hypocrisy that overleaps itself under the garb of
semi-idiotic simplicity; yet I would fain hesitate before
venturing the assertion that Polonius is to be accepted
as the concrete impersonation of Shakespeare's ideal
of a courtier." The only redeeming points in the
career of Polonius are indicated as "The wise precepts
delivered on his first appearance in the play, and
especially so, his advice to Laertes "It is the sole
sound pillar in a rotten building." The article is
worthy of study, as the character of Polonius is
deserving of more attention than it has hitherto
received at the hands of students in the Old World.)

"The Spelling Reformer."

1880. October. "On Phonetic Spellings in Shakespeare," by
F. G. Fleay.

(An attempt to establish the hypothesis that Shakespeare
in the second Quarto of *Romeo and Juliet*, adopted a
system of phonetic spelling, not of course to the
extent of the supporters of this journal. Mr. Fleay
cites many examples, from which a few may here be
given:—Words now levelled under our conventional
spelling in *ed*: accustomd, apparela, poysd, angerd, &c.
Similar words in *t*, levelled under *ed*:—askt, curst,
prickt, &c. Ditto in *de* now levelled under *ed*; preparde,
importunde, rulde, &c. Phonetic writng of *s* for our *c*;
choise, pensill, poultis, &c. Mr. Fleay promises to
refer to this matter again.)

In conclusion; the task I have undertaken in placing before
my readers a selection of references to books, &c., upon the great
Dramatist and his works, with remarks interspersed upon the
nature of the books, articles and views of the several writers, has I
know been very inadequately attempted. The venture is a novel
one and beset with many difficulties; as to accomplish even what is
herein presented, has involved a large amount of reading and labour.
My object is not to give a mere *Bibliography of Shakespeare*; but
the indication to the beginner in Shakespearean study of such
books and articles, calculated to be of service to him, and the
recording of controversies, that have taken place during the past
ten years, which, unless a plan similar to the one here adopted,
would be in the future very difficult to refer to.

Should any of my readers desire to consult to any of the books
or publications I have used, it will give me the greatest pleasure
to oblige him, subject to my time serving.

J. J.

2nd October, 1880.

FACSIMILES

OF

SHAKESPEARE'S AUTOGRAPHS

IN HIS WILL.

SHAKESPEARE'S WILL is written on three sheets of paper, and the signatures occur as follows :—

1.

At end of first sheet.

2.

At end of second sheet.

3.

At end of the Will, which is followed by the Witnesses.

*** The autographs are here given to illustrate the entries of Mr. J. O. Halliwell-Phillipps's books on the Poet's name, and page 5 of *Notes on Shakespeare*.

NOTES ON SHAKESPEARE.

WILLIAM SHAKESPEARE was born at Stratford-upon-Avon, Warwickshire, in 1564, the sixth year of Elizabeth. "*The date of Birth is not known, but was* BEFORE 23*rd April.*" (H) His baptism is recorded on the 26*th* April. From the custom of baptising children when *three* days old, the 23rd April has been *assumed* as his birthday.* His father was JOHN SHAKESPEARE, who, according to Aubery, was a *butcher;* † but is now generally believed to have been a *glover*, from an account discovered by Malone, stating that he was sued before John Burbage, bailiff of Stratford, for £8 as *a glover* (17 June, 1555).

In 1556 he was one of the jury of the court leet at Stratford.

1565. Elected an alderman, when his son William was in his second year.

From Michaelmas, 1568, to Michaelmas, 1569, he served as high bailiff.

Sept. 5, 1571. Elected chief alderman.

1597. Is styled in a deed *Johannes Shakespeare* "*Yeoman*," in the fifteenth year of the poet.

So much regarding the public position held by Master John Shakespeare.

1557. He married Mary, the youngest of at least four daughters of Robert Arden or Arderne, of Wilmecote, in the parish of Aston Cantlowe, Warwickshire. Her marriage portion was a small estate in fee in that parish, called Ashbyes; £6 13s. 4d., and an interest in some property in Snitterfield.

---

* W. Watkis's Lloyd's Life of Shakespeare, in "Singer's *Shakespeare*," p. xviii.

† "Memoir of Shakespeare," by the Rev. Alexander Dyce, pp. i.-ii., and at p. xii., quoting from Aubery's "*Minutes of Lives.*"

Issue of marriage : four sons and four daughters, in the following order :—

Joan, Margaret, William, Gilbert, another Joan, Anne, Richard, and Edmund. The elder Joan and Margaret died in infancy, before the birth of William ; Anne died in her eighth year. Of Gilbert, very little that is *certain* is known. An anecdote refers to his living "to a good old age."* The second Joan married William Hart, a hatter, in Stratford, and died in 1646. All that is known of Richard is that he was buried in 1612-13. Edmund became an *actor* at the Globe Theatre, and was interred in the church of St. Saviour's, Southwark, 31st December, 1607.

William Shakespeare is *supposed* to have received his education at the Free School of Stratford. The age at which he was sent, or how long he remained there, *nothing* is known.† Little can be said beyond mere conjecture about the youth of the poet, until 1582,‡ when, at the age of eighteen and a-half years, he married ANNE HATHAWAY, *supposed* to have been at that time seven to eight years his senior. She was the daughter of Richard Hathaway, of Shottery, in the parish of Stratford.

May 26th, 1583. Their first child, Susannah, was baptised.

Feby. 2nd, 1584-5. Baptism of their twin children, Hamnet and Judith.

From this date *nothing* is known of William Shakespeare's life until 1592, when he is mentioned by Greene, the dramatist, in a pamphlet entitled "*A Groatsworth of Wit bought with a Million of Repentance*," as follows : "There is an *upstart Crow* beautified with our Feathers, that with his tyger's heart, wrapt in a Player's hyde, supposes hee is as well able to bombast out a Blank Verse

* *Vide* "Dyce's Memoir," quoting Oldys.   † Dyce, loc. cit., p. vii.
‡ "Marriage—exact date not known, but was shortly after 28th November, 25th Eliz., 1582." (H)

as the best of you, and being an absolute Johannes factotum, is, in his own conceyt, the onely *Shakescene* in a countrey." The poet's age at this time was *twenty-eight.**

"First appearance in London—date not known."(H) The deerstalking incident and his embroilment with Sir Thomas Lucy cannot be *directly* proved to have taken place.

1593. Publication of *Venus and Adonis.*

1594. Publication of *Rape of Lucrece*, both dedicated to Henry Wriothesley, Earl of Southampton, who at one time gave Shakespeare £1,000 to complete a purchase " he had a mind to," *supposed* to have been in connection with the building of the *Globe Theatre, at Bankside*, by Richard Burbidge. But this is mere conjecture.

The Globe Theatre was commenced in December, 1593. [Built 1599, Halliwell.]†

In 1596, Shakespeare is said to have resided near the Bear Garden, in Southwark, and did not change his residence whilst he remained in London.‡

In this year Shakespeare lost (in August) his only son, Hamnet, in his eleventh year.

1597. At *Easter Term* he bought *New Place*, Stratford-upon-Avon, for £60, about equal to £300 at the present time. Mr. Collier thinks this purchase was made somewhat LATER.

In 1598, Ben Jonson's " *Every Man in his Humour* " is *conjectured* to have been *first* acted by Shakespeare and his company.

1599. Shakespeare became a partner in some of the profits of this theatre,§ and acted in the plays here as

---

* Dyce, loc. cit., p. xxxiii., and Singer's Shakespeare, p. xxxii.

‡ Malone's "Inquiry into the Authenticity of Certain Papers," &c., p. 215.

†§ The Succession of Shakespeare's Plays, by F. J. Furnivall, M.A., 1874, p. xxxviii., being the Introduction to Prof. Gervinus's " Commentaries of Shakspere," trans. by Miss Bunnett.

well as at the *Blackfriars Theatre*. The *Globe* was the *Summer*, and the *Blackfriars* the *Winter* Theatre.

1600, July. Died Sir Thomas Lucy.

1601. Died John Shakespeare, and on September 8th was buried.

1603. At Christmas, Shakespeare's Company performed six plays before the King and Prince at Hampton Court, and received 20 NOBLES for each performance (= £13 16s. 8d.)

1607, June 6. Marriage of Shakespeare's eldest daughter, Susannah, at the age of twenty-four, to John Hall, gentleman, a physician at Stratford.

1608. Died Mrs. Shakespeare (the poet's mother), and on September 9th was buried.

"In my '*History of New Place*,' I have shown that Shakespeare retired to Stratford between September, 1609, and June, 1611. Nothing nearer is known."(H)

1613. Died, at Stratford, Shakespeare's brother Richard, in his fortieth year. In June the same year, destruction of the *Globe Theatre* by fire. Rebuilt at the charge of King James, noblemen, and others.*

1615-16, Feb. 10th. Judith, the youngest and only other child and daughter of Shakespeare, was married to Thomas Quiney, a vintner and wine merchant of Stratford. She died in 1662.†

1616, March 25th. Shakespeare executed his Will.

1616, April 23rd. Died William Shakespeare.‡

As regards the spelling of the Poet's name,

---

* *Vide* the Account in "*Stowe's Annals*," Singer's *Shakespeare*, p. lxxviii., *Pink and Wood's* "*His: of Clerkenwell*," p. 195.

† Singer's loc. cit., lxxxiv.

‡ The cause of his death is supposed to have arisen from the pigsties and other nuisances in the neighbourhood of *New Place*, which gave him a *fever*. VIDE Halliwell's "*History of New Place*," p. 29. The story of the drinking bout with Drayton and Ben Jonson is now rejected from want of evidence. F. J. Furnivall's "*Introduction:*" *Gervinus's* "*Commentaries*," p. xlii.

Mr. (Halliwell) Phillips has sent me the following note:—

"He spells it SHAKES-PEARE in his first work. So do his friends. He sometimes signed himself SHAKSPERE, but sometimes also SHAKSPEARE, as I know by a tracing of the Will made in 1770, before it got damaged. In Shakespeare's time people signed their names in all manner of ways. I have specimens of the signatures of Julius Shawe, Shakespeare's friend, in EIGHT *various spellings!*"

On the other hand, Mr. F. J. Furnivall, the Founder and President of the New *Shakspere Society*, says:—

"This spelling of our great poet's name *(Shakspere)* is taken from the only unquestionably genuine signatures of his that we possess—the three in his Will, and the two in his Stratford conveyance and mortgage. None of these signatures have an E after the K, four have no A after the first E; the fifth I read *eere.**

---

* Vide *The Prospectus of The New Shakspere Society.* p. 5, note 1.

SHAKESPEARE'S PLAYS,*
(*Earliest Editions*).

The First Quarto	...	1597	The First Folio	1623
The Second ,,	... ...	1599	The Second ,, ...	1632
The Third ,,	... ...	1609	The Fifth Quarto ...	1637
The Fourth ,,	...	undated	The Third Folio ...	1664
	The Fourth Folio	1685		

* For a full list of all the Editions and Commentators on Shakespeare, see the "*New Variorum Edition of Shakespeare*," by Horace Howard Furness, Vols. I., II.

NOTE.—"*The Names of the Principal Actors*" who formed the original company: "William Shakespeare : Richard Burbidge : John Hemmings : Augustine Phillips : William Kempt : Thomas Poope : George Bryan : Henry Condell : William Slye : Richard Cowly : John Lowine : Samuel Grosse : Alexander Cooke : Samuel Gilburne : Robert Armin : William Ostler : Nathan Field : John Underwood : Nicholas Tooley : William Ecclestone : Joseph Taylor : Robert Benfield : Robert Goughe : Richard Robinson : Iohn Shancke : Iohn Rice."—First Folio 1623. (Halliwell) Phillips' Reprint, 1876.

CHRONOLOGICAL ORDER and ANALYSIS of SHAKESPEARE'S PLAYS and POEMS.

	Supposed Date.	Earliest Allusion.	Date of Publication.	Doubtful Plays "D."	Plays in which he was not Sole Author.	Remarks.
FIRST PERIOD.						
VENUS AND ADONIS	1585–7	...	1593	...	...	Entd. Stat. Hall 1592.
TITUS ANDRONICUS, touch't up	(?) 1588	1594 M*	[(?)1594]1600	D	...	
LOVE'S LABOURS LOST	1588–9	1598 M	1598 Amended	...	...	
[LOVE'S LABOUR'S WONNE]	...	1598 M		...	...	
COMEDY OF ERRORS	1589–91	1594 M	1623	...	...	
MIDSUMMER NIGHT'S DREAM (?2 dates)	1590–1	1598 M	1600	...	...	
TWO GENTLEMEN OF VERONA	1590–2	1598 M	1623	...	...	
(?) 1. HENRY VI. touch't up	(?) 1590–2	...	1623†	D	...	1622 given by Dyce in his "Memoir."
(?) TROILUS AND CRESSIDA, begun..	...	...		...	...	
(4) LUCRECE	...	1594	1594	...	...	
ROMEO AND JULIET	(?) 1591–3	1595 M	1597	D	...	
(?) A LOVER'S COMPLAINT	...	...		...	...	
RICHARD II.	(?) 1593–4	(?) 1595 M	1597	D	...	
RICHARD III.	1594	(?) 1595 M	1597	D	...	
2 and 3. HENRY VI. recast	(?) 1594–5	...	1623	...	...	2nd pt. printed as The First Part of "The Contention," 1594. 3rd pt. printed as "The True Tragedy of Rd Duke of York," 1595.
JOHN	1595	1598 M	1623	...	...	
SECOND PERIOD.						
MERCHANT OF VENICE (part)	(?) 1596	1598 M	1600	D	...	Entd. Stat. Hall 1598.
TAMING OF THE SHREW (part)	(?) 1596–7	...	1623	...	...	Entd. Stat. Hall 1592, The "Taming of A Shrew" pub. 1604. Acted (?) at Henslow's Theatre, 1593.
1. HENRY IV.	1596–7	1598 M	1598	...	...	
2. HENRY IV.	1597–8	1598 M	1600	...	...	
MERRY WIVES OF WINDSOR	1598–9	1602	1602	...	...	
HENRY V.	1599	1599	1600	...	...	
MUCH ADO ABOUT NOTHING	1599–1600	1600	1600	...	...	
AS YOU LIKE IT	1600	1600	1623	...	...	
TWELFTH NIGHT	1601	1602	1623‡	...	...	Entd. Stat. Reg. 1600. Acted in the Middle Temple Hall 1602.
ALL'SWELL ("Love's L.Wonne," "RECAST)	1601–2	...	1623‡	...	...	
SONNETS	(?) 1592–1602	1598 M	1609	...	...	

THIRD PERIOD.

HAMLET	1602-3	(?)	1603	...	...	Entd Stat. Hall 1602. Acted at Whitehall 1604.
MEASURE FOR MEASURE	(?) 1603	...	1623	...	...	Acted at Harefield 1602.
JULIUS CÆSAR	(?) 1601-3	(?)	1623	...	...	
OTHELLO	(?) 1604	1610	1622	...	...	Entd Stat. Hall 1607. } Acted at Whitehall 1607.
MACBETH	1605-6	1610	1623	...	...	
LEAR	1605-6	1606	1608	...	...	Acted at Court 1609.
TROILUS AND CRESSIDA, *completed*	1606-7	1609	1609	...	part authorship	
ANTONY AND CLEOPATRA	1606-7	1608 (?)	1623	...	...	
CORIOLANUS	(?) 1607-8	...	1623	...	...	
TIMON OF ATHENS, *part*	1607-8	...	1623	part spurious	...	

FOURTH PERIOD.

PERICLES	1608	1608	1609	...	part authorship	Entd Stat. Hall 1608.
TWO NOBLE KINSMEN	1609-12	1614	1634	...	do.	Fletcher & Shakespeare.
TEMPEST	(?) 1610	...	1623	...	...	Acted at Whitehall 1611.
CYMBELINE	1610-12	...	1623	...	...	Acted at Whitehall 1611. Fletcher & Shakespeare.
WINTER'S TALE	(?) 1611	1611	1623	...	part authorship	
HENRY VIII.	1613	1613 (?)	1623	...	...	Acted as a *new Play* when the "GLOBE" was burnt, 1613.

---

* *The letter M prefixed to the above dates refers to* FRANCIS MERES, *who mentions these Plays in his* "Palladis Tamia," 1598, *vide* F. J. FURNIVALL'S *Introduction, p. xliv.*

† *Alluded to by Nash in* "Pierre Penvilesse," 1592. "Could not have been written by Shakespeare, but may have possibly added a few touches." *Vide* Preface to Reprint of 1st Folio, by J. O. (Halliwell) Phillips, p. ix.

‡ *Held* to be mentioned by Meres, as "Love's Labours Wonne," 1598.

₊ The above table is *mainly based* upon the arrangements adapted by Mr. F. J. Furnivall in his Introduction to "Gervinus's Commentaries", and by Mr. C. Knight in "Studies of Shakespeare," edition 1849.

> " *Judicio Pylivm, genio Socratem, arte Maronem,*
> *Terra tegit, popvlvs mæret, Olympvs habet.*"

> " Stay, Passenger, why goest thov by so fast?
> Read, if thov canst, whom envious death hath plast
> Within this monument—SHAKSPEARE, with whome
> Quick Natvre dide: whose name doth deck y^s tombe
> Far more than cost; sieth all y^t he hath writt
> Leaues living Art bvt page to serue his witt."

Obiit Anno Dom. 1616.
Ætatis 53.—*Die* 23 *Ap.*

The above lines are inscribed on the monument in Stratford Church. The date of the erection of the monument is not known, but was before 1623. "The bust was originally painted in imitation of Nature," which was renewed in 1748. Malone caused it to be covered with one or more coats of *white* paint in 1793.[*]

The gentle spirit of the Bard is ever with those who love to hear his name and read his works. These scanty notes are but an earnest of one's love. Language cannot fully express one's feelings, nor convey to another the gratitude that is oft expressed in tears. I will, therefore, conclude with the following lines:—

> " Hearing you praised, I say—'*tis so, 'tis true,*
> And to the most of praise add something more;
> But that is in my thought, whose love to you,
> Though words come hindmost, holds his rank before.
> Then others for the breath of words respect,
> Me for my dumb thoughts, speaking in effect."

Shakespeare's Sonnet LXXXV.

J. JEREMIAH.
URBAN CLUB, 24th April, 1876.

---

[*] Dyce's " *Memoir,*" p. lv., *Note* 79.

ON WELSH NAMES AND LEGENDS OF THE "MILKY WAY." A Contribution to the Study of Welsh Folk-lore. Limited to 100 copies; privately printed, 1871. 8vo. *Out of print.*

ON EISTEDDVODAU; or WELSH MUSICAL FESTIVALS, THEIR ANTIQUITY AND HISTORY. Giving full references to all the leading Works upon the subject; 8vo., 8 pp. Price 1s. 6d. 1876. Only 125 copies printed.

SHAKESPEAREAN MEMORABILIA. Being a collation of all the contemporary allusions to the Name and Works of Shakespeare. Tabulated, 8vo., 10 pp. Price 1s. 6d. 1876. Only 100 copies printed.

NOTES ON SHAKESPEARE, AND MEMORIALS OF THE URBAN CLUB, ST. JOHN'S GATE, CLERKENWELL, with illustrations of St. John's Gate, &c., Portrait of Shakespeare, and facsimile reproduction of the signatures to his Will. 8vo., 140 pp. Bound in cloth, price 5s. 1876.

DITTO, DITTO, Large Paper Edition, revised and enlarged to 170 pp., 4to., containing a COMPLETE collection of Urban Club Poems; a reprint of four scarce poems (Shakespeare fabrications); an account of the Playhouses of the Elizabethan era; a List of the spurious Plays once ascribed to Shakespeare, analysed; a History of the NATIONAL THEATRE PROJECT; besides numerous additions and references throughout the work, the whole forming a comprehensive Guide to Shakespearean Literature. *Printed on superfine toned paper, bound in cloth, extra gilt.* STRICTLY LIMITED TO 50 COPIES, and signed. Price 21s. 1877.

A SHAKESPEAREAN SOUVENIR. Consisting of a Report of the Festival of the Urban Club, held April 23rd, 1877, with addresses by Dr. Westland Marston; Dr. John Doran, F.S.A.; Prof. H. Fawcett, M.P.; and Dr. Schliemann; and the programme compiled entirely from the *first folio*, 1623, with portrait of Shakespeare and a facsimile of one of his signatures, 8vo., 24 pp. Price 1s. 1877.

To be had of Messrs. H. SOTHERAN & Co., 77 & 78, Queen Street, E.C.; Eastcheap, E.C.; 146, Strand, W.C.; and 36, Piccadilly, S.W.